LOOKING BACK

K.C. LONG

PAGE PUBLISHING, INC.
New York, NY

First originally published by Page Publishing, Inc. 2017

ISBN 978-1-64027-640-6 (Paperback)
ISBN 978-1-64027-641-3 (Digital)

Disclaimer: This story and its characters, setting, and plot are fictional. Any resemblances to real names, places, events, or people, living or dead (more likely dead) are strictly coincidental. If you discover anything written in this fictitious story that reflects you or someone you love in any way, shape or form, it is not about you. Even if it is, I'll deny it in court.

Printed in the United States of America

This book is dedicated to
Sharon Fray

CHAPTER 1

The startling ring of the phone screaming out in the middle of the night was something one never gets used to, though it was all too common in the DelGiorno household. Death knows no time limit, nor does it wait until one is ready for it—be it family, friend, foe, or funeral director.

Mr. DelGiorno composed himself, cleared his sleepy throat, and answered the phone in a tone that seemed to say, *"Of course I was awake."*

The familiar voice of the coroner on the other end bellowed as if it were natural to call at this time of night. "Steve," the voice on the phone echoed, "I need you up on Huckabee road for a transport."

Mr. DelGiorno, Steve to his friends, hated coroner calls. They all too often involved more tragic deaths than your standard blue-haired widowed lady living at the local nursing home with a family who had been anticipating her death. Coroner calls were the ones most dreaded by any funeral director. There was no way of knowing what one might find when they arrived at the scene, and more often than not, it was worse than expected—especially the calls that came in the middle of the night. He had seen nearly everything in his career, so nothing much surprised him now, but he still dreaded each tragic call just the same.

Over the years, he had seen many accidents, both vehicular and just plain crazy, like the child who choked on a roasted marshmallow—nothing Heimlich could extract. Or the man who chose to cut trees alone. When the kickback of the chainsaw grabbed his jugular, he was dead before anyone could have saved him, even if he had brought along help. He had seen many suicides and only a few murders he could recall. Of the few Steve remembered, at least two happened in other states. Watkins Glen was quiet, and violent crimes happened only on rare occasions. Even if a local was a victim, often the crime didn't occur in their small town.

One particular case that stuck in Steve's mind was a young boy who had graduated from the area. The boy had moved away and worked as a supervisor at a Christmas tree lot. He was murdered senselessly when a previous employee decided to rob the place and then kill him for having fired him. Ironically, the murder victim had been at the funeral of his best friend just a year or two earlier, and Steve remembered him being very distraught as he threw himself on the closed casket. Steve had since wondered if those two were now together somewhere in the afterlife, best friends again.

The tragic deaths were often the hardest to deal with because in many cases, it seemed to him that perhaps fate could have just as easily changed the outcome. A one-minute change in the timing may have made the difference between life and death for many of them.

Especially with tragic cases, Steve went out of his way to ensure each family was given an opportunity to grieve in their own way, and this was what made him great at what he did. While he offered guidance and direction, so to say, he always allowed families the final say in how the services would be carried out.

As he clicked on the light, he grabbed for his leather tablet and DelGiorno Funeral Home pen that he always kept handy on the tidy nightstand next to his bed. He tried carefully not to disturb the missus, but no matter the time of the call, she too was always awake and unsettled. Each call leaving her wondering how long it would be before Steve would return safely to bed. That was one of the many challenges of being married to a man who was a funeral director.

He wouldn't be home soon either—probably not until morning. By the time he had removed the body, made contact with the family, then embalmed and cleaned up in the prep room, hours would have passed. The peak of the sun would by then be cresting the horizon. It would be a new day for many but not for this person.

As he returned the phone to its cradle, he said a short prayer for the family. This had been a tradition for as long as he remembered. It was something no one else would really ever know about, but it brought him comfort at a personal level, knowing that he had each family's best interest at heart. He combed his bedhead best he could then washed the sleep from his eyes and pulled a freshly pressed black suit and white collared shirt from the closet. He was always thankful that his wife liked to iron even though ironing was a thing of the past for many women. He never had to worry about looking professional when presenting at the scene of the most recent death, calling hours, or funeral.

As he drove to the scene, Mr. DelGiorno recalled how his family from three generations past had committed themselves to this noble profession, but how he still, after all these years, could never get used to, let alone enjoy, being awoken from a sound sleep to attend to a death. On the other hand, the pride of helping a family through such a difficult time was what kept him going, no matter the time of day or night.

He often reflected on how dedicated his previous ancestors were to the reputable name of DelGiorno Funeral Home and how lucky he was to have been afforded such a respected business in his community. It had never crossed his mind, for as long as he remembered, that he might not someday be a funeral director just like his father, grandfather, and great-grandfather. He never wanted anything else. Even though the early morning wake-up calls annoyed him at times, he knew that once he met with each family and was able to bring them some sort of peace during perhaps the most difficult few days of their lives, it would all be worth it.

His mind shifted to his daughter, Kathleen. He and his wife called her Kath, and that seemed to fit her spunky personality much better than the formalness of Kathleen. She was attending the mortuary college in Syracuse right now. Was she tucked safely in bed, enjoying her slumber? Was she free of the worry and burden of death? He often wondered—and tonight was no different—if he should have encouraged his daughter to join the profession. He knew that overall the profession would provide a decent living if she could manage the emotional demands of the job, plus there was great reward in helping people deal with death. It could also be more difficult for her, he reasoned, just for the simple fact that being a woman brought with it more emotion. But he also knew that she would be more compassionate and empathetic toward the families, and that would bring everyone consolation.

He hoped perhaps she would meet a fine mortician at college to marry. Someone to help pull off the night calls when, actually if, he in fact ever retired. All too often, funeral directors went right from the job to the grave without ever having freed themselves from their sworn duty to others. Steve knew this was true, but he still had hopes. Dreams to retire and give his wife a luxurious vacation. One she had never complained about not having but had surely wanted in order to escape the monotony over the years. This business did not allow for time away very often. It was not always feasible to hire or even trust someone else with the never-ending demands of the funeral business, so trips were kept short, close to home, and more often than not, cancelled last minute due to a death call.

CHAPTER 2

The flashing lights ahead gave Steve confirmation that he was approaching the scene, even though he knew the location like the back of his hand. This situation looked grim, worse than usual, he thought, as not only were the police and ambulance crews in response, but firefighters as well. He knew by the look of the mangled-up and charred remnants of the truck it was not going to be pretty. Steve was sure that old Joe the coroner would give him a hand loading the remains, because he would want to go home to bed just as much as he did. After scanning the scene more closely, Steve was grateful it was Joe that was on call tonight.

Joe was an old-timer who was more reasonable and helpful than some of the newbie coroners who went strictly by the book and would never think to stoop to the level of helping remove a victim from the scene. A job that was too "dirty" for them.

As he exited the hearse, he straightened his suit and tie and proceeded toward the wreckage to examine the scene before he would return to the vehicle to retrieve the cot. It was amazing how Steve could transform from a sound sleep to the composed professional in such a short amount of time and still not look as though he had just rolled out of bed.

"What do we have? Anyone we know?" Steve inquired.

All too often, it was. With an immediate population of right around three thousand, this hometown was small and comfortable. Of course, the funeral home pulled much more clientele from surrounding rural towns that did not have their own funeral homes. As a small-town funeral director, part of Steve's job was getting to know everyone in the community and as many people on the outskirts so that on the occasion of death, DelGiorno Funeral Home would come to mind first. The job was not for everyone, that was certain, but Steve was an honest, compassionate man whom families had turned to time and time again, requesting his services in their hour of need. It comforted him to know this as it confirmed he was doing his job and doing it well. He respected the dead and the living, and he was respected in return.

"It is likely a young one. Haven't made final ID yet because he is burned so badly. We are pretty sure it is the Dunfee boy, it's definitely his truck," Joe confirmed.

Chris Dunfee's truck was well-known around town not just for its sharp looks but also because more times than not, you could hear the tires screeching on it somewhere in town. He had restored a 1989 Chevy step-side and customized almost every detail on it, including the 454 engine. Not really a good vehicle for a boy who already loved speed.

He had wrecked the truck on every side since he first put it on the road just a few years back. This even included backing it into a cottage on the lower lake road and leaving a hole in the house. Each time he wrecked it, he'd fix it back up then find trouble again. His dad's auto repair shop made the preservation all too easy, and his father had often bailed him out of trouble because of his bad choices. Perhaps that overprotection had led to his death in some way.

"If you don't mind, I need you to transport the remains to our office for the medical examiner to decide what to do next. I figured the Dunfee family would be calling upon you since their family has used your firm forever. You should be able to pick up the body after it is released, hopefully sometime tomorrow."

Steve DelGiorno didn't mind transporting for Joe, because he would return favors for him often. The medical examiner, or ME for short, was the medical doctor who performed the actual autopsy. Whereas most coroners were only able to pronounce a death. Autopsies were very invasive processes and would often wreak havoc on a body for embalming, but the procedure gave details about death one could not find any other way. Surely they would look into whether or not this victim was under the influence.

"Damn kids never learn. This corner was not made for speeding." Joe continued, almost with anger in his voice.

Was his anger directed toward the twisted corner? Or was it pointed at the irresponsible kid who just ruined his parents' life too? It was probably both, Steve decided.

"Sure hope it was just an accident and not because he was high on drugs or alcohol. Probably pissed at his girlfriend! Thank God there was only one in the vehicle."

Dead Man's Curve was really a little cliché for this corner, because it had taken so many lives over the years. Not just the curve itself, but the two-hundred-year-old oak tree that those unfortunate enough to lose control ultimately slammed into to seal their fate. Those who missed the tree were usually the ones who walked away, but not tonight. This truck had rolled over several times, ensuring the speed was very unreasonable, and then the truck burst into flames. Prior to the curve, the road was so straight that it was all too easy to be going way too fast by the time one realized the corner was approaching. Over the years, they had installed warning signs and bump strips well before the corner, but still there were always at least one or two fatal accidents per year at Dead Man's Curve. This year would prove no different than any other.

Perhaps, if this victim hadn't had a seat belt on, he would have been thrown far enough away from the vehicle to have escaped the fire and his own death. But as it turned out, Chris Dunfee always wore his seat belt. One could only hope that he was unconscious and unaware rather than suffering through the agony of burning alive.

Steve responded quickly to get Joe's mind off his rant. "I'll take care of it. When do you think you will have made contact with the family? I'll need to know as soon as you do so I can get them in for arrangements. Give me a hand, where's the victim?"

The only thing Steve had going for him at this moment was that the accident had occurred on flat land rather than over a cliff or in some gully, and thankfully, Joe was there to assist with the removal. The mortuary cot was not a piece of equipment that was easy to maneuver on tricky slopes. Tonight, at least, Steve was able to effortlessly roll the empty cot over the newly cut grass field. Once loaded with a body, however, he would certainly require assistance to roll the cot back to the car.

As he maneuvered the empty cot toward the wreckage, Steve flashed back to his first solo removal. He had been so proud to be back from the hospital alone. As he turned his corpse toward the ramp that led to the prep room and started to descend, he had forgotten rule number one—feet first. It would be the last time he would forget that rule. So much of a funeral director's training came from making stupid mistakes. Mistakes one could only learn through experience, not in a classroom lecture. As he geared the cot to get headed down the ramp, there was a jolt in his arms then a huge shift in weight as the head end of the body slid down the cot, making it much like an unbalanced seesaw. The cot began to pull forward in a tipping motion. In a brief moment of panic, followed by some quick thinking, he had his arms wrapped around the middle of the cot, hugging the body and hoping and praying the corpse would not go down on its head. This proved a little tricky for a man of his short stature. He was just five-foot six but still the tallest male of the DelGiorno family. Inch by inch, holding his arms tightly around the bagged body, he made his way to the end of the ramp without losing the cargo. What started out to be a two-minute job took almost a half hour.

When he finally emerged from the basement, the pride of his first removal had become a lesson in cot protocol. He returned to the funeral home office and inquired why his dad had not come to check his status after he had taken so long. He was miffed, but it really wasn't his dad's fault. He had assured his dad before he had left that he would have no problem accomplishing the task, so why would his dad have been concerned? It was probably for the better that he was not caught because the embarrassment of having made such a rookie error would last much longer than the resentment he felt toward his father at that moment.

Joe's concerned voice brought Steve back to reality. A place he decided he'd rather not be after his senses began taking in even more of the horror at the scene. Most sights didn't bother Steve much after these many years in the business, but there was nothing that would prepare you for the smell of charred human. A bittersweet mix of a Hawaiian pig roast and singed hair.

"We're going to have to be real careful with this one. Not sure how well he is going to hold together, being charred up the way he is. Almost like cooking BBQ till the meat falls off the bone." A description that was true but not necessary to say out loud.

"I've got a disaster bag, why don't we try to put that under and use it for a lift? It will be easier than trying to just pick him up. Plus, if we lose a part, it will all be contained in the tarp."

"Sounds good. I am in no mood for collecting body parts tonight."

Mr. DelGiorno quickly returned to the hearse to retrieve the bag, and he grabbed his flashlight as well to provide a little more illumination at the scene. The soft breeze carried the charred smell all the way out to the road, taking some of the edge off the burnt hair scent. Maybe those who weren't present at the scene would perhaps mistake it for a meal grilling in someone's backyard, except it was the middle of the night. He doubted anyone would be cooking at this hour.

The job went smoother than expected, and no limbs were lost among the living or the dead. Both of them were even able to keep their composure as they turned the body side to side in order to place the bag under it before lifting the remains onto the cot. They were extra careful not to press too hard in any area, for fear of putting a finger or hand straight through the skin. The ME would probably not even remove the body from the bag, just to keep everything intact as much as possible. There wasn't going to be much they could do for an autopsy, but because of the traumatic cause of death, the body had to be returned to and then released by the ME before a death certificate could be issued.

Joe helped in every way he could. He was a good egg, and Steve knew he chose to help on removals because he too would have wanted the same respect if it were someone in his own family. That was what drew people to these strange professions. The idea of helping others and taking pride in knowing that at the end of the day, they had brought some good to what otherwise was an awful situation. Good that often no one else even realized one had done. Not too many people were cut out to do that type of work. It took empathy—lots of it—and one had to be okay with not receiving recognition for everything they actually did behind the scenes.

Joe had been a coroner almost as long as Steve had been a funeral director, and Steve appreciated Joe's attention to detail and willingness to help even though his actions and words could at times be a little rough around the edges.

With their team effort, they finally managed to get the corpse safely back to the car. The seemingly thunderous bang of the hearse door closing rang out a finality that went unspoken, as if to say, "Here it is, the last ride."

"I'll be getting a hold of you just as soon as we have made contact with the parents!" Joe reassuringly shouted as he handed a paper to Steve. "Why don't you take the death certificate to the ME to save me a trip? It might get your body released a little sooner."

As Steve carefully began to drive away from the scene, he instinctively used his side mirrors to guide his moves. After thirty years of working and even longer growing up in the funeral business, he had never looked in the rearview mirror when transporting a corpse. There was just something eerie about it to him. He never wanted to catch a corpse sitting up, staring at him in the mirror. A quirky and unrealistic fear, he knew, because in all the years as a funeral director, a body in his care had never moved—ere it were due to gravity—even though there were many wives' tales to refute that. Quirky indeed, but Mr. DelGiorno was a bit of a quirky man.

CHAPTER 3

The morning sun peeked brightly through the window of her apartment. Only two more days until graduation, Kathleen thought with anticipation. As she lay in bed, trying to shake off the night's sleep, she contemplated whether or not she should stay there a little longer or seize the day and make the most of it. Having a father in the funeral business gave her a peek inside the value of hard work but also reminded her that sleep was essential, and one should take it when they had the chance.

There weren't any classes today, but her classmates, all fourteen of them, were getting together to study for the National Board Examination scheduled for tomorrow. Each year three classes graduated from Simmons Mortuary School. Graduation ceremonies occurred in January, May, and September with usually no more than fifteen students or so in each class. This exam was her last big step before her yearlong residency with her father at the family firm, then she would be a licensed funeral director.

She often wondered if her dad had ever felt disappointed that he had not had a son to pass the business on to. After all, he was the fourth-generation son to take over, and he would now have to leave the family business to his daughter. A hundred years ago, it would have been nearly unheard of, and surely her great-great-grandfather would have never pictured, or likely approved of, a woman funeral director. Although her dad never let on that he was disappointed or felt that way, she often questioned it in her mind. She doubted it though. After all, he had even swayed her to attend the same mortuary college that had been his alma mater, but only after he insisted she earn her business degree first.

Her dad wanted to be sure she had more than just the certificate you earned in mortuary school. That way, if she decided on changing careers later, she would have a degree to fall back on. A smart choice, she realized now, because she could not picture herself having been ready to be a funeral director at nineteen. At twenty-three, with five years of school under her belt, she had experienced life outside of her little hometown and was ready to embark on her career.

She had toyed with the idea of becoming a social worker, but she could not come to terms with her family having to sell the funeral home someday. In recent years, many small family-owned firms had been bought up by greedy corporations, more often than not for much more than they were worth, and then most ended up closing. The blue-collar bigwigs hadn't figured out that you couldn't put a funeral in a can and sell them the way corporations wanted. They were all about profits, but a real funeral director knew that there were circumstances and situations where profit was not the only motive. A good director could still make a decent living providing quality goods and services for the deceased and their loved ones without resorting to underhanded corporate tactics.

Anyway, funeral directing was a close second to social work, as both professions were about helping others get through rough spots in their lives. People often didn't realize that more time was spent with the living than the dead in the funeral business.

No matter, her fate was sealed. Graduation was just two days away, and there was calmness in knowing that she would be returning home to the town she loved to continue on the traditions her ancestors had laid down before her, even if she was a girl. She looked forward to adding her headshot to the wall of funeral directors depicting each funeral director in charge since the home had opened, including her great-great-grandfather and his brother, the original founders of DelGiorno Cabinet Making and Embalming.

She always thought it made sense that those who built cabinets would also build caskets—a cabinet for the deceased, hence turning to the business of death. Back when the family business was started, one could apply for an embalmer's license at the town hall. No education required. The founding DelGiorno's had learned carpentry from their father, who was a tradesman, and they had helped a local funeral director as children. They did odd jobs around the funeral home, and in turn, he taught them the trade. Eventually they took what they knew about both trades and began their business in Watkins Glen, New York.

The name had since changed to DelGiorno and Son Funeral Home after her own grandfather joined the business. Building caskets on site had gone by the wayside; however, the history remained, and she was becoming a part of it. Other than the name and various aesthetic and functional changes to the interior over the years, the house itself remained mostly the same. It had been painted white with black shutters since the very beginning. A large covered porch with a brick base wrapped around the front and north side of the building. It was a place where families had gathered time and time again before entering to say their final farewell to their loved one. A place of retreat in order to get away from the crowd for a few moments to compose oneself or to completely break down.

The original heavy oak front door with a large oval glass insert and the screen door with a *D* in the center of the scrolling still remained. The door and oak moldings that graced the building's unique structure were handmade by the DelGiorno boys who first opened the funeral home, clearly showing their talents as master craftsmen.

Up the grand staircase were the living quarters, though the door that led inside their home had been locked sometime ago. During some other funeral home updates, they had built a private entrance. Now, the living space was accessed through a hallway in the back of the funeral home that connected the business to the personal space. From the hallway in back was the entrance to the kitchen, which had been just a large screened-in porch. It was converted years ago so Kathleen's mom could easily bring out food to entertain her family and guests by the lake frontage that bordered the rear of their property. A newer set of stairs led to more living space upstairs, including a sitting room with a fireplace and bedrooms for Kathleen and her parents.

There was also a small mother-in-law apartment upstairs. If she wanted more privacy, Kathleen would be able to move her things over there, but for now, she figured she would be just as comfortable in her old bedroom. She had no real reason to need a lot of privacy but could always make that choice if she wanted more independence sometime down the road.

She was so much looking forward to her parents coming to town for graduation and dinner. As she drew closer and closer to graduation, she became more confident that her parents were very proud of her decision to carry on with the family business.

As she anticipated her parents' arrival and approval, her mind soon shifted to what she would wear to the ceremony. Most of her outfits consisted of something black, which would be appropriate for the event, but she wanted to be a little more girlish for this day as opposed to the typical boring look of a funeral suit.

Keeping tradition with the DelGiorno stature, Kathleen was a petite girl with a perfect smile. She looked good in almost anything, but she was smart about not letting that go to her head. She was modest and down to earth and in no way arrogant about the fact that she was beautiful. The mix of her father's olive Italian skin and her mother's reddish Irish hair gave her a fine combination of features that would captivate anyone who laid eyes on her. As she matured, she began to really appreciate these features that added to her beauty, something that wasn't so easy as a child growing up. Back then the kids teased her about her red hair, but now she had definitely grown into it.

The knock on her bedroom door caused Kathleen to snap out of her daydreaming and make up her mind about getting out of bed.

Her roommate, Chelsea, was hoping they could catch some breakfast and then meet up with everyone else to study for their exam. Upon Chelsea's request to join her, Kathleen realized she was starving and popped out of bed to start her day. Thankfully, she and Chelsea had burned significant calories as they exercised to *Buns of Steel* the previous night, so she was in dire need of bacon. Bacon gave her just the incentive she needed to get ready in record time. Plans for a graduation outfit would just have to wait.

CHAPTER 4

The phone call from the ME brought some relief to Mr. DelGiorno. He knew that the hold-up in releasing the body would enable him to postpone the funeral long enough to ensure he could attend and enjoy Kathleen's graduation. He would then be forced to break the news about Chris's death to Kathleen, but not until after Kath had a chance to enjoy her accomplishments of the day. Her first funeral as an employee would be someone she knew. This would be something that would become all too commonplace as she continued in the business.

A twinge of regret again swept through his mind as he wondered whether he might have pushed her into the wrong profession. Would she be able to handle the pressures of daily death looming over her? He reassured himself she could; after all, she had been around it since she was a child, but the burdens of daily death sometimes took a toll, and he had kept her sheltered as much as possible for the beginning years of her life until she could better understand death. Would she turn cold like him, putting one's own feelings on hold to tend to the feelings of others? Only time would tell.

Steve recalled the day of his own beloved grandmother's death. Sure enough, his mother called to inform him in the middle of a funeral ceremony taking place in his own chapel. He remembered his mind racing between feelings of grief, wanting to break down, and the knowledge that he was not able to do so, not when someone else's grandmother was lying in wake in the chapel in the next room over. Someone's grandmother died every day, but other people didn't experience this knowledge and were by nature allowed to grieve at death. Not a funeral director, though. It was almost as if he had to force himself to recognize a death in his own family because it became so common that Steve felt as if he could not be selfish enough to grieve when others were grieving too. He found this to be the most difficult aspect of his job.

He never did go to his grandmother's-out of-town funeral because the families who chose his funeral home needed him. The blur of the commitment to his own family and the duty to client families began to become less clear. He never had forgiven himself for missing her funeral, even though he knew that there was nothing he could have done for Grandma by then. The funeral was, after all, for the living, and he had living to attend to at his funeral home.

He shook himself out of his self-loathing and went on to find his wife, Jules—short for Julie. Her friends had assigned her that nickname after Demi Moore starred in *St. Elmo's Fire*, and it stuck after all these years. He was eager to share the news about the body being held up, because although she hadn't mentioned it, he knew it would be weighing on her mind. Too many times before had plans been changed, events been cancelled, feelings been hurt in his family to ensure the client families' needs were met. They would be going to graduation no matter what. He had also confirmed coverage with a nearby friend so that they could spend the night and have no worries about being called back unexpectedly.

Every independent one-man operation funeral home had someone they trusted enough to help out in a pinch and to ensure they could get away when necessary. Usually it was someone a town or two away so that they were not in direct competition with those covering.

For DelGiorno Funeral Home, the go to man was Roger Dugo. Steve and Roger had actually been friends since they were young boys because Roger's and Steve's dads had shared the same conveniences for coverage over the years. He owned a funeral home two towns over in Bath, about twenty-five miles from Watkins. It worked out well, but you could only ask for coverage occasionally or lose your connection for good. Now and then, they might also arrange for one another to work a larger funeral in order to drive a second vehicle to transport family members to the cemetery. No money usually exchanged hands because it was a barter system; no one took advantage, and no one really kept track, but when something came up, they could count on each other to be there as long as the schedule made them available.

As Steve entered the room, he felt Jules's tension and was grateful that her edginess subsided when he confirmed the good news.

"I've lined up Roger to cover our trip to Syracuse for Kathleen's graduation. I just talked to Joe Mantiono," he continued. "There are issues at the office in getting the body identified for release, so we will be free to enjoy her day without having to worry about the Dunfees wanting the funeral the same day."

While her heart went out to the Dunfee family, she couldn't help but be relieved that their current situation would not be cause for her to miss her own daughter's celebratory day. A newfound blush rose to her cheeks, indicating her relief. It highlighted her beautiful reddish-blond hair and striking green eyes that had first drawn his attention to her. Her features were delicate compared to the Italian features of his aunts, mother, and cousins.

"Have you spoken to Donna or Tim?"

"Not yet, I needed the confirmation from Joe that they had been notified."

Just then, the phone rang. He was quite certain that it would be someone from the Dunfee family, and sure enough, it was. He was eager to get them in for arrangements today so they could leave on time Saturday for Syracuse. This would give him plenty of time to write the obituary and have it in for the deadline and hopefully file the death certificate before they left town. There would be no viewing in this case, which would save a lot of time, but he couldn't help but imagine how terrible it would be for the Dunfees to realize that they would never get a last look at their son. Their only memory now was of whatever he was doing the last time they saw him. He hoped that it was a good memory.

Any accident was difficult for Steve, especially anytime people were involved that were near the same age as Kathleen. More times than not, the closer to Kathleen's age they were, the more likely he knew both the victim and family well. It reminded him so clearly about how short life was and how quickly it could be taken away, even when it was least expected. He knew that if he were in that situation, he would have a difficult time, and this connection helped him to be more considerate toward what the family would need. Nonetheless, he hated being reminded that any time, any day, he could be faced with a loss of one of his own family members. He often wondered how he would react if he were on the other side. He doubted he would lose it completely, at least not in public. He had been trained, although not intentionally or by any master tradesman, simply from experience, not to overreact to death.

If he was lucky, the body would be released by early tomorrow so he also could have the body prepped before departure too. Prepped? What prep? This was a true case of tag and bag. Embalmed only with external powder then pouched, which would hopefully tone down the inevitable char smell that was sure to permeate through the funeral home if not properly contained. He would have to steer them toward a metal casket with a seal if they were not choosing cremation.

The wood casket was too porous to make a difference, and although the funeral home had just one other burn victim, that family's choice of casket had made it impossible to keep the remains in the front room. Mr. DelGiorno had to explain to that particular family that he would place the empty casket for visitors, because there was no way to have the body present and not evoke a smell no one would be able to forget. Perhaps the Dunfees would just choose cremation; their son was practically there already.

CHAPTER 5

J ules couldn't help but notice what a lovely day it was to be celebrating graduation with her daughter. As the light breeze fluttered, the smell of fresh lilacs and lake water were permeating through the bedroom window. They had planted that tree when Kathleen was just small, and it now nearly reached the second-story window, allowing for the scent to waft in easily. She couldn't help but notice how quickly things grow up, including the tree and her daughter. She wondered where the time had gone.

The May air was crisp and refreshing, and the sparkle of the morning sun rising over Seneca Lake was the one thing that had kept Jules sane through all the years of no vacations or getaways. At least the funeral home was located just off the lake, and she spent many days relaxing away from the house, where the end of their big backyard met the lake.

There she could pretend she was on a tropical island or in the Florida Keys and could escape both the sadness and feeling of impending doom the funeral home often carried. She enjoyed having friends and family over to share the lake, forced to entertain at her house so that Steve could be close to home to answer the phone if needed and leave promptly for a death call. While they couldn't leave their home often, the lake's beauty and serenity was enough of a "getaway" for her, and she was grateful to have this beautiful large home on the lake, even if part of it was so closely attached to death.

She had met Steve in Syracuse when he was at mortuary school. She attended a local community college for secretarial science, but she didn't really like it. It was just what many girls were expected to do.

The local hangout in her neighborhood, which was close enough to the mortuary school to also attract the crowd of future funeral directors, was where she first laid eyes on him. Swallows was a quiet bar, just a place to grab a burger and a beer and get away to relax a bit, which was why she liked it. She was quiet and relaxed and fit the scene well. At Swallows, there were no rowdy drunks or wild parties—except for the three weekends a year during Simmons graduation when the class would celebrate hard their rite of passing to the real world of death.

She often wondered how they did it, if they really would like their jobs and why in the world anyone would want to do such a thing. That was until she met Steve. She was quite smitten with him and found that although the thought of him being a mortician was a bit creepy, he was indeed a very kind and caring person. Much different from the stereotypical dark and lonely funeral director kind she had imagined all her life. Not that she thought much about funeral directors. Her only experience with death up until that point had been at her grandmother's funeral a few years before they met.

She remembered being rather disturbed by the very tall all-in-black man standing somberly at the door, a bit of a Lurch-looking character with hardly any personality, and she had kept thinking he would pop up behind her and say, "You rang?"

Steve was quite a different man from her vision of funeral directors. He was very attractive with his dark, almost-black neatly trimmed hair, which was now spattered with touches of gray, making him even more distinguished, and brown almond-shaped eyes with beautiful long lashes. She didn't mind he was a little on the short side; he still was a few inches taller than her, so she could get away with wearing a small heel without feeling like she towered over him.

He had lots of charisma and had such a true kindness about him it was no wonder he felt compelled to help others. They dated off and on while he attended school, but when he finally brought her to the lake to meet his family just before his own graduation, she was sold. She knew right then that she could not live without him or that lake lot. She loved his mother and knew she could teach her even more about cooking. Her homemade Italian meals and cannoli were to die for. Jules always got a kick out of hearing stories about the troubles Steve would cause his mother as a child and how he got his not-so-Italian first name.

She would make do with her doubts about being trapped in the death business as long as she could spend afternoons near the lake. He had told her many times that she would not have to work, but she could surely help with the bookkeeping because of her experience in the secretarial program.

Soon after they married, they moved in the very small apartment in the back for a few years until his parents decided they could better manage in the smaller apartment. Steve was eager to produce an heir to take over the business when he was old. It took them a few years to get pregnant, which finally gave them their beautiful daughter. Steve never got a son, as once Kathleen was born, Jules was told she had cancer and was in need of a hysterectomy to rid her body of the disease. He never complained about not getting his son to carry on the DelGiorno name and quickly grew fond of the idea that his daughter might someday take over.

Finally, the day had arrived for them to work side by side until he would gradually release the reins to her, as his father did to him. Jules was glad that the world had changed enough from when she was attending college to allow her daughter to make that choice. Kathleen surely wasn't the secretarial type. It would truly be a special time, and Jules couldn't help being proud of her daughter.

As she reminisced, she hurried to get around, knowing that the phone could ring any instant, and they could be delayed. She wanted to get on the road right away before anything or anyone could change their plans!

CHAPTER 6

The trip on the I-90 was better than they expected. They had escaped the funeral home earlier than planned, and traffic conditions were on their side. The weather continued to sparkle all the way there, and the anticipation of seeing Kathleen grew stronger as they approached exit 39. They had not visited her often in Syracuse, not just because it was hard to get away from the funeral home, but Kathleen had been away to college for a long time now, and they did not feel the need to hover over her. Kathleen would pop in to visit her grandmother, Jules's mom, at the assisted living facility. Knowing they both had company in each other made Jules feel okay about not visiting either of them too often. Anyway, they were all able to keep in close touch through cell phones and text messages.

Cell phones were a luxury not afforded morticians when Steve first entered funeral directing. He either had to be tied to a wall phone or a pager and answering service, which were finally reasonably priced a few years after he started in the business. Now with call forwarding and cell phones, Kathleen would practically have free rein and be able to do much more than the DelGiornos ever could. This brought both her parents some piece of mind, knowing that her career would include a much less restrictive life than theirs had been. Steve's father had had it even worse. If someone couldn't phone sit right at the funeral home and know exactly where they could reach old Mr. DelGiorno, he would have never left the house for fear of missing a call. It was life consuming then, and still was, but with a little longer leash.

The graduation ceremony was short and modest. No graduation gowns, no long valedictorian speeches, just a defined group of individuals who were making a commitment to serve the public in a noble profession. Jules couldn't help but notice that Kathleen looked strikingly grown-up in her outfit. Although it was black, it was a shimmery material with a knee-length skirt and a slightly low-cut front. It said professional but fun—which was a perfect description of Kath.

The mirror behind the group of students allowed for the audience to see both the front and back of each outfit. Kathleen's mother found the back of Kath's outfit to be as beautiful on her as the front. She could see by the detailed clips on the back of her swept up hair that she had taken much care to look just perfect today. Her mom was almost certain that Kathleen was grateful she had not had to wear the usual graduation mortarboard cap that would have ruined her hairdo and taken away from her overall beauty.

Following the awarding of diplomas, the graduates collectively read the Funeral Service Oath while raising their right hands.

A copy of this oath hung neatly matted and framed in the front entry of DelGiorno Funeral Home. Mr. DelGiorno silently read it along with them while following the words on the program and intermittently glanced proudly at his daughter as she vowed the words:

*I do solemnly swear, by that which I hold most
sacred:*

*That I shall be loyal to the Funeral Service
Profession, and just and generous to its members;*

*That I shall lead my life and practice my art in
uprightness and honor;*

*That into whatsoever house I shall enter, it
shall be for the benefit and comfort of those bereaved;*

*That I shall abstain from every voluntary mis-
conduct and corruption;*

That I shall obey the civil laws;

*That I shall not divulge professional
confidences;*

*And that I shall be faithful to those who have
placed their trust in me.*

*While I continue to keep the unviolated, may
it be granted to me to enjoy honor, in my life and
in my profession, and may I be respected by all men
for all time.*

A roar of applause filled the room, and the newly hailed
graduates were eager to put on their party. The DelGiornos had not
had much time to speak with Kathleen before the service, so they
filed out to greet her again and passed along hugs and well wishes to
the few other students they had come to know.

Chelsea and her parents would be joining them for dinner.
Although their parents had not met before, Kathleen and Chelsea
wanted to celebrate their last night in Syracuse together. They had
grown very close throughout school, having been the minority in
their class.

Chelsea was not from a funeral family but had found an
internship close to home through a family friend. She was relieved
because it was difficult enough to be a woman in the business but
even more so if your family didn't own a firm. In fact, Kathleen's
father had helped Chelsea by allowing her to visit the funeral home
a couple of weekends in order to complete the required embalmings

needed for graduation. She needed to work most weekends in order to attend school and had a hard time fitting in the embalmings otherwise since she didn't have family in the business. She may or may not have actually completed all of them, but the paperwork was in thanks to Kath's dad.

Dinner was also a quiet affair. Kathleen and Chelsea laughed with their parents as they thumbed through the yearbook memories. It was a first yearbook in many years at Simmons. Thankfully, a parent of one of their rich classmates had agreed to finance most of it after a few fund-raisers the class had were a flop. Kath and Chelsea were the editors and were quite proud of their production.

Everyone at dinner got a rather morbid laugh from the last few pages, where each of their classmates were on display, laid out in caskets. Pictures that were taken after they had snuck into the showroom at school and posed for their mugs. All looked pretty creepy, except Sullivan—he had decided on a nice urn for his photo.

The imprint at the bottom of the page "Thanks, Mr. LFD, for allowing us to use your facility" was a bit of an apology to the dean, who got an earful after it was discovered that the students had actually broken into the showroom and tore the interior of the expensive casket as each of them climbed in and out for the photo op.

They continued to share stories about other photos in the yearbook of parties at Dr. T's house and the house across from the school, where most of the boys lived. They reminisced about the pictures of their trips to Batesville and Marsellus Casket companies for the big tours to encourage them to buy their products someday. Chelsea and Kath looking so professional in their suits on one tour but rather ridiculous when you panned to the safety glasses on their faces.

Mr. DelGiorno admired how Kathleen and Chelsea got along so well and thought back to the many friends he had met and forgotten about during his time at mortuary college. His only connection to anyone from that time was, of course, Jules and Roger, who had also attended college at about the same time as him. Steve also shared stories that evening, recollecting strange events that had happened over the years, much to Kathleen and Chelsea's amusement. To her surprise, Kathleen had not heard many of his stories before and was glad to see that, at times, he really could relax and not take everything so serious.

His greatest story was his description of a great misfortune he encountered at a burial one day. He explained how he had just finished carefully placing each family member in a seat near the grave and instructed all the pallbearers to be extra careful after having been warned by the cemetery personnel that the hole was unstable. It had to be dug much larger than was usually necessary due to the wet ground caving.

Just as he walked around back of the grave to begin services, down into the grave he tumbled. He explained that once he realized he was unscathed and luckily missed injuring himself on the concrete vault on the way down, to cover his embarrassment, he jumped out of the grave exclaiming, "Ta-da!" Being with his very conservative father and seeing his beet-red face, Steve described how he wasn't sure if his father was about to implode in anger or explode in laughter. He explained he never did find out how his dad felt about his act and never tried to find out either. No matter, it was a story that was too hilarious not to share. He insisted he would never be able to forget the day he was almost buried alive while trying to bury Chet Decker. Everyone at the table laughed to the point of aching bellies and near tears.

Kathleen didn't know her grandfather well, but from what she had gathered over the years about him, she thought he most likely had not approved of her dad's little stunt. She knew for certain she and her dad would also probably butt heads a time or two themselves but hoped the stories would turn out to be fun memories later.

With all the shared stories, the night seemed to end far too quickly. Kathleen was glad that her parents were there to drive because while reminiscing with everyone, she had easily drunk a bottle of wine or more. This, of course, made her a little teary-eyed as everyone parted ways because Kath knew deep down that she and Chelsea would probably not keep in close contact even though they were inseparable this past year. They lived hours away from each other, and both would be busy getting their careers started. It was the way life worked. When those close to you were out of sight, gradually it would become easier to forget about them. A sad fact that was part of human nature, but Kath was going to make an effort to stay in touch anyway. A promise she hoped she would keep.

CHAPTER 7

As Kathleen awoke, her head was pounding a little, and it took her a minute to realize just where she was, but quickly she became alert to the surroundings of the hotel. The way-too-matched pink, blue, and seafoam-green curtains, carpet, and bedspread were sure signs of well-planned decorating to the point of nausea. The hotel was definitely a little outdated, but still they had the Sleep Number beds, so she slept well. She reached above the bed to twist the switch on the wall lamp in order to provide a little more light. She must have passed out almost as soon as she hit the pillow, as she was still in her slip and bra, and the TV was on. The curtains were never closed either, something she always made sure to do at hotels to ensure her privacy. Thankfully, she was on the top floor.

Her parents had reserved a hotel because the girls had to be out of their apartment by yesterday or be forced to pay another month's rent. She was sure her parents wanted their own room because they so infrequently got away. No big deal to her, given the fact that she was obviously not in very good shape last night and lay practically naked on her bed.

She was eager to get home, enthusiastic to make contact with a few old friends that were still in town, and ready to see the lake once again and relax with her mom. The weather was getting warmer and the days longer thanks to daylight savings. It was a new beginning for her, and it reeked of goodness.

Her parents were already knocking on the door, probably ready for breakfast, so she quickly covered up with her discarded shirt from last night. As she cracked the door with the safety latch still engaged, just in case it was a stranger, she found her dad standing there.

"Good morning, Ms. Funeral Director." He beamed.

"Not as good as it could be with this headache. When's breakfast?"

"Mom and I will be ready soon, but I needed to speak to you about something before we get home."

"What is it, Dad?" She could tell by his face that it was not good news.

"Wednesday night we got a funeral call for a friend of yours." He hesitated briefly to try to soften the blow slightly. "Chris Dunfee was killed in a car accident. We have the call, and we will be holding the calling hours tomorrow. I just wanted you to be expecting it when you get home. It will not be easy, I know."

Kathleen was a little surprised she hadn't heard yet. Her dad had not even thought about the possibility of her finding out through Facebook. But luckily, Kathleen had been so tied up in studying for her national boards she had basically shut off all her technology to ensure she stayed focused.

The news stymied her eagerness to get home. Now those feelings were replaced with dread, but this was the life she chose, and living in a small town, she would have to get used to knowing the deceased. She just hadn't expected it so soon or for it to be one of her best friends growing up.

She immediately flashed back to the crazy times they had in high school. Dead Man's Curve, nearly wrecking after a keg party at Skyline. He was driving too fast, as most teenagers did on that road, but all six passengers in the four-seater car came out unscathed, and no one else ever even knew once they got the car back on the road. She thought about how Chris was always the life of the party.

"What happened?"

His eyes lowered as he tried to think of a way to shield her from the horror, then he just blurted it out. "He was driving too fast on Dead Man's Curve off Huckabee Road. He burned to death in his car."

She would know all the details soon enough. He reasoned that she would have to get used to it. He couldn't protect her anymore, not from death.

She was a little startled by the fact that her mind had gone directly to that place when his name came up, and yet that was also where he had died. They had been to so many different places because they had hung out so much during high school, why did she move to that particular place and time? It was almost as if she knew more than she had realized. She quickly chalked it up to coincidence and then scooted her dad out so she could cry in private without looking weak.

As he left, he apologized for not telling her sooner, but she was glad he hadn't spoiled her graduation day with the news.

CHAPTER 8

Although the ride home from Syracuse had been a little gloomy, Kathleen woke up early on Monday morning eager to get to work helping her dad prepare for the calling hours. She knew it would be busy because younger deaths always brought in huge crowds. Even when someone wasn't popular (but Chris was), there would be the gawkers and the "I am pretending I was their friend crowd," who usually cried the hardest for their own narcissistic attention.

As she popped out of bed, she could smell the distinct scent of seaweed and fish, which was actually a somehow pleasant scent of the lake out back. For a brief moment, it took her mind from the miserable day ahead to great times when all her friends would gather at the dock to swim and tan. Chris was always the jokester and at all times kept the crowd laughing. He was always looking for that last high school party, one to beat the last one, and never lacked for someone to hang out with. She was glad she could still picture him in her mind, as now she would never have a chance to see him again.

Chris was a weightlifter, a real jock who, if he wasn't careful, would start to look like a pinhead when he lifted too much. His blond wavy hair and blue eyes were appealing, but although he was cute, he was not drop-dead gorgeous. All the girls considered him more like a brother than someone you might tentatively create a long-term relationship with. He put himself in danger often, probably to impress the girls, but that was the exact behavior that usually kept them at bay.

Really, for all the off-the-wall danger he often put himself into, Kath found she actually was surprised he lived this long. She also doubted that the autopsy results wouldn't indicate some illegal substance in his body, but then again, maybe it was pure adrenaline that made him drive too fast around the corner he should have known better about. She wondered how the ME would even extract the necessary blood to send for analysis. They must know how to do it; she figured maybe through tissue samples or something. Based on the fact that he was bagged and casketed when she arrived home, she knew that there hadn't likely been much left to work with but was perfectly fine with not knowing for sure.

Facing his parents later was going to be rough. She and Chris had a brief fling in high school, and he took her to the senior prom. But it did not last long. And who knew who else might show up that she had lost contact with since college. Some she would be glad to see, others not so much. Regardless, it would be a sad time, not a time to reminisce or make new connections, which she had originally looked forward to doing upon her return to town.

One o'clock came quickly. Although calling hours did not start for the public until two, it was common to be ready at least an hour early to give the family their own personal viewing time prior to the public. Today there was nothing to see. Yes, there were lots of flowers, and for sure, the family would bring pictures that would need to be placed around the room to keep the collection of people from overwhelming one area of the chapel, but there was no body to see, no hands to touch, nothing but a cold metal box. The family insisted that he have a traditional burial and a Catholic Mass at St. Mary Our Mother followed by a burial right next to his grandmother's grave, who was currently on the near-death list at the local nursing facility.

Kath's dad had made her prearrangements a few months ago, so the Dunfees had just said to match Chris's services to hers to ease all the decisions that went into planning a funeral, and even worse, planning a funeral for your child. Decisions that some lingered over for hours, while others knew right away what fit their loved one. Each family and service was unique in its own way. Some families insisting on the most expensive, others the very least expensive, and many making choices strictly to match the taste of the deceased.

Caskets weren't the only decisions to make; burial or cremation, what cemetery, what clothing, what to put in the paper, what time to have services . . . the list went on, and as Kath checked off all these things in her mind, it was a wonder that the process of funeral arranging didn't take much longer. A good director, who could read families well, usually took about an hour and a half at best. She knew it would take her a while to get the routine down, but her dad was an expert. He knew what to say at just the right time, how to present the more difficult topics, such as cost, and when to keep talking or when to be silent. He had a charisma that people were drawn to that clearly cemented the trust between him and the families that he served. Even though it wasn't scripted, after so many years of meeting with families, if you had listened in at each set of arrangements, you would have believed he had been reading from a teleprompter behind them.

Doors began slamming out front, people were filing out of vehicles, some crying, and others were carrying pictures, many holding hands, waiting for Mr. and Mrs. Dunfee to approach the door first. Showtime.

It was a bittersweet day for Kathleen, it being the first day working as a real funeral director, an achievement she had worked hard to accomplish. Yet a day she would help to bury a friend. She wasn't sure whether to laugh or cry, but she did neither, just tried to stay composed.

The first set of hours was a mob scene, people crying—sobbing, rather, in and out for cigarette breaks. The sea of people was almost overwhelming to Kathleen, but her father stayed his calm self, reassuringly greeting people at the door as if to say, "It's okay, just come in and be taken care of."

Kath was surprised she had not seen more people she knew, but then again, most of them probably worked, so they would be more likely to come during the evening hours. Actually she was relieved, because up until now, she was able to keep her emotions in check but knew if the right person arrived, she could easily slip into hysterical crying like all the other grieving visitors. Showing emotion was something all experienced funeral directors usually learned to curb, and she knew she would need to toughen up or risk looking like a fool. It was an unspoken rule that the director in charge of arrangements would not turn to a babbling ass at someone's funeral. Tricks like visualizing something funny in your mind, blowing your nose, or rolling your eyes and swallowing the hard lump in the throat to hold back tears sometimes worked, and she was using all of them today.

CHAPTER 9

K athleen's dad had taken her mother on an errand between
calling hours, so she promised she would hold down the fort
until they returned. She was glad they were not gone long
as it was barely seven o'clock when a line again began to form at
the door. It was definitely going to be a long night because once
there was a line at calling hours, it usually meant it would be at least
several hours before everyone got a chance to weave their way to the
receiving line. Ironic that it was called the same for a wedding—
although in each you are receiving guests, the circumstance for which
you form one are polar opposites.

Kathleen was glad she had had a few hours of reprieve after
the first set of hours and had enjoyed her first home-cooked meal.
Mother always had dinner waiting for her dad following a set of
calling hours. She did this not only because he would soon need to
return to work but also to ensure he would have the energy to stand
the next set hours and tackle whatever else he might have to attend to
until the next mealtime arrived. He had missed tonight's meal, which
was not common, but Kathleen was happy to eat his portion.

About an hour into the second visitation, Mr. DelGiorno remembered he had picked up a personal item of Chris's from the coroner's office but had left it in the hearse. Although somewhat blackened, his St. Christopher metal had surprisingly beat the heat and had been given to the funeral home with his personal effects envelope. Sensing Kathleen could use a break, he asked her to go to the garage and retrieve it. He was sure the family would be grateful that it was still intact and decided he would present it to them at the end of the evening.

Kath couldn't have been happier to move away from the door and collect her thoughts. As she opened the door to the hearse, a strong scent of new-car leather filled the air, and she sunk into the soft gray seat just to relieve herself of the pain her heels were giving her from standing in one place too long.

Her dad had just purchased the new hearse a few months earlier. She let out a deep sigh and pulled the key back from the ignition to eliminate the annoying *ding, ding, ding* that told her the door was open, then she laid her head on the rest. The odometer lit up to read just two thousand miles. Over the years that would tick up well beyond as they made trip after trip to hospitals, house removals, and burials.

She just needed a few minutes to collect her thoughts, and she would be ready to go back. She practiced her yoga breathing, something she learned from Chelsea when they lived together during mortuary school. It helped them relax after a bad case at school.

The school had its own trade service, which usually meant that most of the calls were those other firms did not want to embalm themselves. Kids, decomp cases, accident victims, more often than not, the worst of the worst. The lady whose cats began to eat her after dying unattended and remaining there several days, the ivy-leaguer who wasn't quite bright enough to know that going down a chimney would get you killed. Then of course, there was the poor guy who had dropped dead and landed with his face on top of the heat register. After lying there for days during nearly the coldest time of the year, all that was left of his head was now in liquid form in the grate. The stench at the school was so offensive, even after completing as much disinfecting and preparation as possible, she imagined the house might never be habitable again.

Because of all the odd cases, Simmons prep room was a great place to learn the trade, or art, rather, of body preparation. Embalming and restoration was an art. In fact, along with embalming class, there was a course called Restorative Art. She laughed a little to herself when she pictured the RA head that she had created. She still needed some practice in this area but knew her dad would be a great teacher.

As part of the class, each student had to rebuild a model head from a special restorative wax complete with true facial features and hair. They were graded on a variety of things, including how the hair was inserted to appear to be growing out, not just placed on top of the wax. She had cut her own hair to use it for her model head. To really make it look authentic, it involved individually inserting one to two hairs at a time, like a hair plug from the Hair Club for Men. She did not fare well in that category, too much time.

She remembered being intrigued by learning the secret to the facial feature measurements—the eye was the same width as the nose, nostril to nostril, and the lips double that. An ear's length the same as the lip's width. She often wondered, who had ever figured this stuff out? Maybe the old cadaver robbers. Promptly following completion of class and receiving their grades, a bunch of classmates took their heads to an old field for target practice. Another great stress reliever, she had learned about at school.

There were the practical jokes too. One day a group of students found a collection of old glass eyes and dentures that had been retrieved from personal effects and unclaimed over the years. There were many a days when everyone would be gathered in the student lounge only to be disturbed by someone gagging and fleeing as they reached the bottom of their coffee, and they found an eye staring up at them. Needless to say, Kathleen never left any drinks or food unattended in the lounge fridge, just for safety purposes.

Just as she nearly dozed off, the interior light dimmed, and even though they were closed, her eyes noticed the change to darkness, jarring her memory that it was not time for bed but time to get back out to calling hours. She clicked the overhead light back on, and as she glanced into the rearview mirror, she clearly thought she had seen an image of Chris's grandmother. Startled by the face, she quickly found the personal effects envelope and went back to work.

She was back at the door for only about fifteen minutes when the phone rang. As if their day had not been long enough, now they would probably be getting another call. The phone didn't usually ring this late at night except for such occasions as death. Her dad went to retrieve the call, and she continued to stand the door, greeting the weary visitors. Kathleen noticed an old pal a few callers behind who had come to pay his respects. He had also been in the car the night she and Chris had gone off the road at Dead Man's Curve so many years ago.

She was surprised that she hadn't seen more of her high school friends, but realized that those still in college were probably unable to leave, since most campuses were in the midst of finals for semester end. She often missed friends over holidays because the schedule at mortuary school was slightly different from most colleges. She had three full semesters instead of just the usual fall and spring, so her breaks were short.

As she waited for her dad to return with the news from the phone call, her friend reached the door. "Johnny, so good to see you," she said, her voice indicating she was relieved to see someone she knew. It would be good to talk with someone a few minutes to break the monotony of standing the door, and since the line was moving pretty slow, she would have a minute to talk to him.

She had forgotten how handsome he really was. It had probably been since her first year in college that she had seen him last. In high school, he had long hair, although it was well kept, but his new shorter cut brought out his features in a way she had never noticed before. Johnny was a member of the old clan, and they had spent many a day together at the lake or bumming around town for shits and giggles. It was refreshing to see a familiar face, someone that took her mind off the sadness of the evening.

It wasn't long before her dad emerged, but instead of coming to her to give her the details of where the removal would be, he walked directly through the crowd to Mr. and Mrs. Dunfee. Kath could tell by their reaction that this was not going to be good.

Mr. Dunfee cleared his throat. "Excuse me, friends and family. Excuse me."

Within a few seconds, people began to hush and focus their attention to him.

"Ladies and Gentlemen, we are so gracious that you have come to support our family this evening. We have just been informed that Chris's beloved grandmother has passed at Clear Rivers, and I must leave to go to my mother. I hope you can all understand our predicament, and we thank you all for your kindness and consideration of our circumstances at this time."

Kath felt the blood rush from her face, and she nearly fell over from the news. Was that whom she really saw just minutes ago in the mirror? Luckily for her, Johnny was still standing by and grabbed on to her just as her knees were about to give way.

Snap out of it, Kathleen. You are a funeral director, soon to be head of this operation. You cannot lose it now! She scolded herself internally.

"Are you okay? You look like you just saw a ghost." Johnny chuckled

"No, no, I am fine. It has just been a long day and . . . and I am just stunned by how awful it must be for the Dunfees. What are the chances of this?"

"Maybe Chris helped her get there. Maybe it was her time to go so Chris would not be alone."

Sensitive, she thought, but not likely. Death just happened in her mind. There was no explanation or planned time. Yet she could not get the image of Chris's grandmother that she saw in the hearse out of her mind. She remembered his grandmother, and she was pretty sure the image she had seen was her. *No,* Kath contemplated again, *maybe I'm just over tired from the exam, graduation, and then a long first day of work.*

Because several of the members of the Dunfee family were preparing to go to see Grandma, the crowd began to disperse some. As each new person arrived for Chris's visitation, they were told of the situation with the Dunfee family by the next person in line or someone else passing by. Of course, many knew her too, and it became a double shock. Some left without even going to the closed casket, knowing they were really only there to see the family; others signed in and still went to say prayers over Chris's casket.

Johnny stayed at Kathleen's side, and she was relieved to have a friend to lean on for a few minutes. She tried to make small talk to keep her mind busy, but she also was truly interested in what he had been up to, so she pried a little.

"Well, I have recently been appointed to a county coroner position here in Schuyler County, and I work as a firefighter too. I was glad I hadn't been on call as the coroner or for the fire department the night of Chris's death."

Nobel professions, she thought, but hardly what she had expected. Her dad had mentioned that many of the newer, young coroners were arrogant and worthless. She was hoping he was not referring to Johnny. She was sure that Johnny would have been considerate enough to assist her dad on a call if necessary. In fact, he said he was just appointed, so perhaps her dad hadn't even been aware of his new job.

They talked for quite some time before they both realized that they were practically the only ones left in the building, even though it was just barely nine o'clock. Once the Dunfees had to leave, no one else had much reason to hang at the funeral home. While she felt terrible for the family, Kath was somewhat relieved, as it had already been a long night. A night that wasn't over because as soon as Clear Rivers called to let them know the family had left, they would need to make a removal immediately.

The facility did not have a morgue, so the nursing home needed funeral homes to be prompt. If for some reason a funeral director could not make it right away, unfortunately for the deceased, the custodian closet became their temporary home. That had always infuriated Mr. DelGiorno, so whenever possible, he ensured he made prompt removals at the facility no matter the time of day.

A state-of-the-art government-funded facility when it was built, with a broom closet as a makeshift morgue. Surely someone in the bureaucratic chain of command must have realized that people in a nursing home were going to die, and a morgue would be a necessity, but not in this case. It would be more humane and much easier to make a removal if they would just leave the deceased in the bed, pretending they were sleeping, until the funeral home could arrive.

The phone rang again, which was Johnny's cue he had better be leaving. Mr. DelGiorno appeared to confirm that they needed to head to Clear Rivers.

"Kathleen, now that you are back in town, can I get your number to keep in touch?"

She handed him one of her new business cards that her dad had printed up and presented to her with a brand-new cell phone and number as one of her graduation gifts. She was thankful to have them handy, so she did not miss this opportunity to stay in touch.

"Good night, Mr. DelGiorno."

"Good night, Johnny, drive safe, son."

CHAPTER 10

Kathleen was catching a second wind and feeling good about going on her first removal with her father. The new car smell of the hearse made her feel even more important. She was anxious to show him what she had learned at school and how independent she could be to help ease his mind about her working with him.

As they drove, she asked if he had known about Johnny's new position at the coroner's office but was glad to learn that he was unaware. This meant that Johnny couldn't possibly be the one that her father often complained about in disgust. She was hoping that Johnny would call her sometime, and knowing that her father did not have some predetermined grudge against him would make things much easier if she did decide to meet up with him sometime.

Once they parked the hearse at the back door of the nursing facility, Kathleen insisted on maneuvering the cot, still her dad kept a close hand on the other end mainly because he knew the layout of the place much better than her. The service elevator was the one they had to use to get to the correct floor. No sign of death at these places. If a death occurred during the day, they all but locked everyone in their rooms to shield them from the inevitable. God knows you wouldn't want any of the old people to realize that someone had actually died in this place. Might cause an uprising, a revolution, refusal to eat, or maybe they would all make a pact to poop their drawers at the same time on a Monday afternoon. At least by this time of night, most everyone was already asleep and in their rooms, which would make this job easier and swift.

The elevator was archaic compared to the rest of the facility. It was almost like they wanted you to feel trapped in a dungeon so maybe you wouldn't come back. The metal doors actually had to be hand manipulated. First a screen-type enclosure then two heavy metal doors that were pulled with handles far too close to the middle. One wrong move and you could pinch your fingers easily. Once the doors were jarred to begin closing, they moved on their own, and one needed to be sure to move all traces of hands out of the way before the doors slammed shut. Only three buttons existed: floor 1, floor 2, and the basement. Being trapped there for a few seconds made Kath believe the architect of the facility had been tweaking final costs, so they left out the morgue and found a used elevator on eBay.

When they reached the second floor, Mr. DelGiorno halted the cot in order for him to ensure no residents were in the hallways. He didn't figure there would be any this late at night but knew that he would not hear the end of it if Betsy, the night supervisor, caught him rolling a cot by a resident. He gave Kath the all clear, and she confidently strolled out, ready to conquer the task at hand.

All went smoothly as they arrived at the room, and when Kathleen saw that old Mrs. Dunfee had actually gained some weight since she last saw her, she was glad her dad was along. No matter how determined a girl might be, the upper-body strength needed to lift bodies was just not as useful in women as it was in men.

Her dad used utmost care in wrapping and moving his client from bed to cot. He made darn sure he tightened the belt straps around the body and reminded Kathleen of the importance, a crucial lesson learned from his near mishap on his own first removal. Had those straps been a little tighter, that body would have never slipped as far or as fast, causing that cot to want to dive ass over teacups. Funny how even though the incident happened so long ago, it only took once for him to know what not to do ever again. He wondered what lessons Kathleen would be unfortunate to learn on her own and which, with his guidance, he could help her avoid due to his own previous inefficiencies.

Even though death loomed in the room, he relished the moment because it would be the last time he and Kath would be on their first removal together. As they turned to leave, Kathleen caught a glimpse of a photo of Chris and his grandmother, which evoked the words that Johnny had spoken earlier, and she thought to herself that perhaps her death was meant to be so they could be together. That made her feel a little less sad for Chris; surely there would be great parties in heaven, if that was where they were.

The ride home was uneventful, and Kath and her dad discussed how ironic the turn of events this evening had been. Mr. DelGiorno could only recall one family, other than accident victims who died together, who had been in a similar situation. It was a man and wife, Phyllis and Don Glasgow. It was believed that the husband died just a few hours after his wife of a broken heart. They had calling hours side by side and were buried exactly fifty-two years after they were married.

It was funny how Mr. DelGiorno had so quickly recalled their names, but when dealing with families, there were always many who became permanently engrained in part of the memory. Perhaps it was because of something unique about their service, but usually it was just because for a few days of life, they became a part of his family until the services were over. Maybe part of the duty to serve and respect the dead was also to remember.

As Mr. DelGiorno put the car in reverse and began to back toward the garage door, he thought better of his plan and decided that if Kathleen pulled the cot out first, they would have more room to unload. It would make it much easier than trying to maneuver in the already tight garage. After all, he now had a second director.

"Kath, hop out and take Mrs. Dunfee to the prep room. Then I can back the hearse in. It will give us more room."

"No problem, Dad."

She jumped out with such a fury to please he knew having her home was going to be a good thing. The rear door clicked open, and then a thunderous crash ensued at the back of the hearse. Mortified, Mr. DelGiorno luckily remembered to put the car into park and ran to the back door. In her haste, Kathleen received her own first lesson in what not to do on a removal. "I forgot to release the legs!" A necessity she should not have forgotten.

She practically spit on him trying to hold back her laughter, as the cot lay neatly on the ground below the hearse bumper, its stainless steel legs and whirly wheels neatly tucked under it like a sleeping cat. Except for the one wheel still spinning aimlessly, everything was still.

"Thank God it is dark out here! What the hell would the neighbors think?" he said as the laughing pains began to flurry up his rib cage. "This is why we always secure our load," he reassuringly stated to make his point about the importance of fastening the belts around the body.

They barely got through the embalming without cracking up every time they made eye contact. It was still just as funny when they retold the story to her mom in the morning.

Kathleen was stricken with an odd feeling when she reentered the prep room that morning. She wanted to check on Mrs. Dunfee, make sure her features set well and there was no leaking. When she had opened the door, the image she had seen in the mirror the night before came flashing back. Now with Mrs. Dunfee embalmed and restored to her more natural self, she was absolutely sure this was whom she saw last night.

Now what? Kathleen thought to herself as the phone began to blare. *Hopefully not another funeral call.* She figured they would be tied up with Chris's funeral until at least late afternoon. The out-of-the-ordinary ringtone made her realize it was not the funeral home phone but her cell. She reached for it, noticing it was an unfamiliar number.

"Hello?"

"Kathleen, it's me Johnny. I, um, I took the day off for the funeral today and was hoping that you might be able to have a cup of coffee or something when it is over?"

The pause on the other end made him rethink his invitation, but her pause was from butterflies rather than a reluctance to accept his offer. "I mean, it was just really great seeing you last night, and it has been such a long time. I was hoping we could catch up. You know we all promised to keep in touch when we went our separate ways for college and jobs. We owe it to each other."

She was a little overwhelmed by her excitement; after all, she had never had any feeling for Johnny in high school, but the sincerity in his voice made it hard to say no.

"Yeah, I think that sounds great." She tried to act slightly less excited than she was actually feeling. Play hard to get and you will land your man. "I will have to deliver flowers after the cemetery. Maybe you could go with me and help."

"Sounds good. See you then."

As she turned her attention back to Mrs. Dunfee, she was reminded of her previous thoughts before the phone call. *God, girl, you are exhausted, overwhelmed with all that has happened, and you need to put it out of your mind,* she reasoned. Surely she really hadn't seen her in the mirror. *Why would Mrs. Dunfee have appeared to me?* she wondered. She left the room abruptly and headed for the shower so she could be ready for the funeral Mass on time.

CHAPTER 11

Kathleen and her father pulled up to the front of the massive gray brick church. Mr. DelGiorno was in the lead with the family car. Kathleen carefully followed in the hearse and eased her way toward the curb, trying hard not to bump the tires, thus leaving marks. Mr. DelGiorno was very meticulous about the appearance of their livery and surely would not approve of gouges in the sidewalls.

She preferred to follow her dad as he had all the best routes carefully planned from the funeral home to church then church to cemetery. He knew which lights he needed to cautiously get traffic stopped at to allow the rest of the procession through and which intersections they could more easily just glide through due to light passage of traffic. Kathleen was touched when an elderly man had taken the time to stop his walk and place his hat over his heart while he watched the procession go by. It was barely possible to get drivers to be considerate enough to stop, but that was a true gesture of kindness and respect for the dead when a man stopped on the street. She wondered why her own generation had become so self-indulgent.

Even though there were several churches in the area, this was one of her favorites. She loved the architecture and large-style bricks that made up the front. Even the chiming of the bells was her favorite tone. They had rung on the hour when she attended the Catholic grade school across from the church. She had always clicked her tongue along with the chimes every time they rang. As she parked, she pictured herself and Chris playing hopscotch or jump rope on the front lawn of the school in their tidy uniforms. Even though Chris was wild, at least at playtime he always avoided any activities that might gain the nuns' attention and cause them to end recess early and force all the children to say prayers.

Her dad had already come to the church earlier to place the No Parking signs outside in front. It was a good thing too, because the street was lined with cars, and the parking lot was overflowing and backed up. He had also delivered a few select pieces of flowers that would stay behind after the service. The rest of the flowers were carefully packed in the hearse, closest to the front seat to be taken to the cemetery.

All the other flowers that were still at the funeral home would need to be picked up, loaded in the hearse, then delivered around town later. She looked forward to having Johnny's help for more than one reason.

The pallbearers gathered at the hearse, and by following the discreetly whispered words under the direction of Kathleen, they passed the handles along to the bearer ahead. Then when each had hold, they lifted simultaneously to move the casket from the car to the vestibule. There it was lowered down at her command onto the church truck, which was the rolling cart that carried the casket. With Kathleen at the lead, her father at the back, and the bearers—three on each side—they slowly rolled the casket feetfirst, resting just inside the sanctuary. Entering feetfirst was tradition. In case of the resurrection happening at that very moment, the body would be facing the altar.

They waited quietly for the priest to come to bless the casket with prayer and holy water before covering it with the pall. The pall was to cover the entire casket so that all who entered were given equality in the eyes of God, and it always matched the robe that the priest wore. Just as the first bell chimed ten o'clock, the typical time for Mass at their church, the priest emerged from a small room on the side of the altar.

The service was mostly a typical funeral Mass, but was made more personal with several prayers and a touching eulogy spoken by close friends and relatives.

When the funeral ended, they turned the casket to exit feetfirst, representing a parishioner leaving, then began the procession back down the aisle. It was always a nerve-racking time for the directors to make sure everything went smoothly. First turning the casket and then directing the pallbearers from their seats to once again accompany the deceased. Then they would slowly begin the procession back down the aisle while ensuring perfect timing for the lead director to stop the casket briefly so that the end director could instruct the family to follow.

Funeral directors never wanted to make a mistake or look as if they did not know what they were doing. But really, when a mistake was made, usually it was only the directors who knew simply because they attended so many funeral Masses. Most of the public were just happy to follow their lead, not really having a clue what was supposed to come next.

As they walked, Kathleen scanned the pews to see if she could spot Johnny in the crowd, but to no avail. After a final blessing, the pall was folded, usually by the funeral directors but this time by the pallbearers, finally the doors were opened and secured to allow for the casket to be swiftly loaded in the car to avoid people standing around, talking. This removed any chance of them being late to the cemetery.

On this day, as Kathleen cracked open the doors, the sun was gleaming and the sky blue. She felt sorry that Chris would not be experiencing this beautiful day, at least not here on Earth. There were kids playing in the schoolyard across the street, and the happy voices of the children along with the birds chirping struck her as an odd reminder that life went on everywhere else today.

Once the car was loaded, Johnny emerged from the church. He walked with such confidence Kathleen was glad they would be spending a little more time together getting reacquainted. Since they needed to leave quickly for the cemetery, Kath was unable to speak to him but gave a brief wave as they both entered their vehicles.

The cemetery service was short and touching. Kath was eager for it all to be over so she could finally talk to Johnny. Following the committal, Johnny drove his car to the funeral home. Once there, they loaded the hearse with flowers for deliveries and were on their way. When they had finally dispersed all the flowers to the local hospitals and nursing homes, Kathleen felt more like a cocktail than coffee.

"What do you say we head over to the Ice Bar instead? I could really use a drink after today."

"Sure, I didn't know that flower delivery could be so demanding. A beer sounds good right now."

Kathleen was thinking something a little stronger would be needed, but she would make that decision when they got there. She thought she might indulge herself in one of their specialty martinis. She loved the chocolate-covered cherry, more of a dessert than a drink. It really felt like you were drinking a chocolate-covered cherry, one of her favorite treats. A combination of cherry and chocolate vodkas and instead of the usual olive in the bottom, a plump maraschino cherry was left to devour after soaking up the goodness of the alcohol.

"Let's drop off the car and walk over to town. We don't need to be drinking and driving especially in a hearse."

She knew if she got started on the martinis, she would likely be in no shape to drive.

A few hours and many cocktails later, Kathleen's light-headedness was telling her it would probably be best to go, or she might find herself in a heap at the bottom of a barstool sooner than later. After they had arrived and had their first casual cocktail, a few other friends from high school had had the same idea following the funeral, so it was a bit more of a party than either of them had initially expected.

"Do you think I could get a cute young gentleman to walk me home?"

He looked around, pretending to find a cute dude to walk her home, then replied, "I'm afraid if I don't, you might not make it. Let me get our tab."

"Oh, and you pay for the date too? How nice."

She knew that she was letting the booze talk now. She had hoped it was a date, but she did not want her play-hard-to-get cover blown. She just tried to ignore what she said as if it never happened.

She needed to sober up fast because she had promised her mom she would cover phones for them tonight so her parents could get a long-deserved evening out together. She would not feel too good if she had to spoil their night just because she couldn't hold her liquor. "Hey, how about that cup of coffee you promised me this morning? I'll buy."

They began the short walk back to the funeral home, making a quick stop for two mochas on the way. Kathleen was glad to have Johnny there to help her stay upright.

As they entered the funeral home, Johnny realized his phone was missing. "Remember, you were talking on it in the hearse? Did you use it after that?"

"I don't think so, let's go check."

As they entered the garage, Kathleen fumbled for the light switch. She was really just getting used to the layout of the area again, having been away to college for so long. She leaned against the hearse, while Johnny searched around the passenger side. "I don't see it. Can you try to call my number?" Really, he had found it but wanted to be sure she had a record of his number on her phone without looking too overzealous.

She reached for her phone, pretending to be irritated with him, and started to dial but quickly realized she had no idea who she was dialing. "What the hell is your number?" she said in a teasing voice.

"607-338-3000."

The phone began to jingle a hokey fire siren noise. "Oh, I can see you take your firefighting job seriously," she jested, torn between whether it was a bit tacky or just plain cute. "Even your ringtone is alarming."

"Yeah, indeed I do take my job seriously," he snapped confidently. "Don't firemen make you hot?"

Their puns were getting competitive, so she thought carefully about her response. She was a little slow on the return even though her first thought was *Hell yeah, you turn me on.* "Well, even if they did, what makes you think you'd be the one to ring my bell, Johnny?"

"Probably because I am so cool. Don't you have a burning urge to check out my hose?"

She guessed he had used this lame pickup line before but still thought it was clever. She tried not to let him know though, so she turned her head as she giggled a little to herself. The flirtatious tension was filling the room with trepidation as each wondered who would make the first move. To her relief, Johnny gave in quickly, and as he slid out of the car, he pretended to stumble a little and fell toward her. She was eager to grab him but still felt it was necessary to not look too eager just yet. As his face moved in closer to hers, she could barely contain her desire to latch on to his robust lips. He pressed his lips on hers, and she could taste the distinctness of the beer on his breath. Still, he tasted good, and his warm tongue slid past her lips and playfully danced around.

He grabbed hold of her almost violently, but in a way, that made Kathleen want to scream out with pleasure. She reached behind her to grasp the door handle leading to the back of the hearse. She knew the layout of the hearse would provide lots of room, but the casket rollers would be hard and cumbersome. She didn't care; her goal now was to get him inside and take full advantage of the situation. It had been a long time since she had been intimate with anyone. She craved his attention.

Kathleen's mind went briefly to her parents. Hopefully they wouldn't come home at this inopportune moment. She wondered if they had ever been so risqué, but surely not before they were married. Good Catholics didn't partake in such behaviors. Her mind quickly snapped back both because it was not fun to imagine her parents having sex but, too, because she had much better things to be concerning herself with at this very moment.

She had gotten away from attending church much after she went away to college, something she knew would have to change in order for her to continue to build connections in her community. At least for now, her separation brought her less guilt as she returned her mind to her desires for Johnny. She would confess these sins later.

Johnny delved his hands deep up her skirt, trying to release any fabric that was causing a detour to him getting his flesh on her flesh. She was delighted that her job required her to wear skirts, at least today. He was gentle but brisk with his movements, showing both that he was a gentleman but one with needs. She tried not to look too desperate and, for as long as she could, restrained from helping him undress her.

Finally, she could no longer hold back the urge to assist in the process. She tore back his shirt then went straight for her own buttons. By now, both were nearly bare, with only remnants that would not hinder their final penetration. As she ground her pelvis toward his groin, she winced with both pain and delight. Her knees bore down on the hardness of casket rollers, but at this moment, she did not care, as the pleasure far outweighed a bruised knee.

As she arched her back to grind harder, her eyes caught a light through the tiny glass window partition between the front seats and the casket cabin. She moved more swiftly and again was stricken by a glimpse of light in the front seat. She was so engulfed that she never even thought it could be her parents. She focused her eyes toward the light, which seemed to come from the rearview mirror, and a clear image of her neighbor Mr. Thomas glanced back at her. Startled, she looked around, thinking he must be at the back of the hearse, but nothing. Johnny sighed as he took her quick movements to be an intentional part of the sex.

When she glared back toward the rear of the hearse, clearly no one was there. She figured that her cocktails were contributing to her unwelcome vision—or hallucination, rather. She pressed harder to orgasm and lay down exhausted but satisfied on Johnny's chest.

CHAPTER 12

Kathleen woke with more than just a headache the next morning. She ached between her legs, and her knees were throbbing. It took her a minute to recall that the pain she was experiencing was all due to a wild night she had instigated all on her own. She couldn't remember what time Johnny left or even saying good-bye to him. Her mind switched to relief that no calls had come in overnight, as she surely would have been in no shape for a removal.

She moved slowly in order to control both the pounding in her head and the aches and pains in other areas. As she inched toward the kitchen, she was hoping to find some ginger ale and something with lots of carbs. A loaded cheeseburger and crispy fries sounded great but was not likely something her mom had prepared for breakfast. As she walked little by little down the stairs leading to the kitchen, she could hear that her parents were awake.

"He's been sick for some time. It is probably a blessing to his family he has passed," her mom was commenting as she entered the room.

"Who are you talking about?" inquired Kath.

"Mr. Thomas died at home last evening. You slept through the phone call, so I decided not to wake you," her dad sheepishly responded. "Did you have a rough night?"

Kathleen's thoughts quickly moved to last night and the vision she saw in the hearse. Her already queasy stomach began to rise up in her throat not just because she had drunk too much but because she was sick about having predicted his death. Why was this happening to her? Was she willing these people to their end?

She ran toward the bathroom and immediately began heaving the entire contents of her guts, nearly missing the sparkling white bowl. *Fuck . . . what the hell is going on?* Her mind raced with a variety of possible reasons. As she dry heaved once more, she was again reminded of the joyride she had taken last night, as the muscles in her thighs and crotch coiled against the pressure of her body pushing down against her abdomen to release more bile. Her esophagus burned, and she swallowed the saliva forming in her mouth in hopes of reversing the flow.

She was embarrassed that she had missed a house call but relieved she did not have to remove the body of someone she had perhaps willed dead. Her mind continued racing. Was her father disappointed in her behavior? Did she and Johnny remember to get all their clothing from the back of the hearse, or did her father find them? She wondered if she could stay locked in the bathroom for the day and try to forget about all the guilt she had because of all her bad choices over the past twelve hours. She had only been home a few days, and already she felt as though she was coming apart at the seams, literally right now.

She vowed she would go to confession very soon. Maybe there would be a penance that would rid her of these horrible visions. And she would never drink again, probably. She gargled with some Listerine and nearly crawled out of the bathroom.

"Dad, I hope you didn't have trouble making that house removal alone." She spoke in a low voice that begged forgiveness. "I am really sorry. After we delivered the flowers, we went for one drink, but many of my old school friends were out after Chris's funeral. Things just got a little out of hand. I promise it won't happen again."

She knew that house removals were tricky even for the most experienced crew, but going on one alone was not a good idea as you never knew what problems might arise. The worst scenarios, of course, came to her mind immediately, like narrow halls and stairways; families standing, watching your every move; and even worse, trying to move a body alone with no lifting equipment.

"No worries, honey. The family's nurse was there, and so was Joe. I knew her well enough to ask for her assistance, and as usual, Joe was always ready to help. But next time you plan to go out, please make it on a night Mom and I will be home. If we hadn't walked in the door when the phone rang, I don't think you would have come out of your coma to answer. We could have lost the call."

He was exaggerating a bit because the Thomas family had been close to their family for years. There was no way they would have chosen another funeral home; they just would have waited to reach her dad. Kathleen still felt guilty and knew she needed to pull her head out of her ass if she was going to make it in this business. She hoped her dad did not need her to sit in on arrangements today. She needed to return to bed and try to forget about her troubles.

"I need to lie back down. Dad, will you need me for arrangements later?"

"I don't think that will be necessary. Mr. Thomas had prearrangements, but after you rest awhile, plan to get Mr. Thomas prepped for services tomorrow. Several of the family members must leave town to get home soon, so they want to expedite the services. They've already been here a week."

"I got it. I just need a little shut-eye and a long hot shower, and I should be back to my old self."

She glanced at her mother, hoping for a reassuring vote of confidence, but her Mom's eyes were engrossed in the morning paper, probably to avoid the awkwardness that was taking place between her and her father. Kath slinked back to her room and lost herself in blissful rest.

CHAPTER 13

By the time Kathleen woke, she felt much better, and after her shower, which was extra long and hot, she was completely renewed. She picked up her phone, hoping that Johnny would have texted, but nothing. She had a lot of making up to do to her father, so she went straight to the prep room to begin the finishing touches on Mr. Thomas. She remembered that her dad had mentioned that he was sick a few weeks before she had returned from school. The family had called to make some preliminary arrangements and had asked her dad to check on him often. He was happy to oblige.

As she pulled back the door, she was taken aback by a second body lying on a cot next to Mr. Thomas. Another call must have come in while she was asleep, which needed to be embalmed. She would prep Mr. Thomas then get right to work on the next cadaver to help make up for the fact that her dad was working double time to cover her ass. She figured he was upstairs, making arrangements with the Thomas family. If he returned and she had completed enough work, he wouldn't be able to stay mad at her. She flicked on the old radio for ambiance and went straight to work.

She turned to find two sets of clothing hanging near the prep room door. Must be the nursing home had sent clothing along with the latest call to save the family a trip there. This man was surprisingly young to have been in a nursing home but obviously had been quite ill based on his emaciated features. She figured he must have needed long-term care due to a terminal illness or something.

She grabbed a handful of paper towels and carefully turned Mr. Thomas to each side, wiping the prep table and his back to make sure there was no leftover moisture or blood that would soil his clothing. She began rummaging through the white grocery bag to find the undergarments to get started. She giggled to herself as she pulled out a leopard thong, but who was she to judge people after her disgraceful evening.

She used several tricks she had learned at mortuary school or seen her dad do to make the dressing process easier. Undies, socks and pants first, picking up one leg at a time and shimmying the waist of the garment side to side until it reached proper position. T-shirt, always both arms in first, pulling tight up over the shoulders until the stiff arms almost lifted, then the collar could be pulled and stretched over the head with ease. It wouldn't matter if it was overstretched as it would not be seen in the end. She carefully cut the dress shirt and suit coat up the back, knowing that each edge of the cut would be neatly tucked behind him to appear as if he had been dressed in an intact suit. Mr. Thomas was now coming together nicely.

Cosmetics were her favorite step. She enjoyed this because the Lyf-Lyk-Tint was a way to bring a slight color of life back to the face which was lost when all the blood was drained from the corpse. It was thin and, well, lifelike. Much better than the cakey clown-like makeup some of the old-time funeral directors preferred. Nothing said dead like a heavy fake makeup look.

She meticulously brushed the tint over every inch of white skin that was still peeking out from his clothing. Face, neck, inside the ears, under the nose, on his hands, even between the fingers. After all, the goal was to make them look alive, not dead. Finally, color on the lips, a coat of powder, and a last check over to remove any loose brush hairs, and he was ready for casketing then viewing. Mr. Thomas looked peaceful and natural, as if he might greet her once again in his friendly voice.

He had always had a beautiful garden, and when she was about ten, Kathleen started spending many hours helping him plant and harvest, just to have an excuse to be outside. She loved bringing home fresh vegetables to her mother to see what she would create.

Kath pried her mind away from her memories to force herself back to work. In order to embalm the next corpse, she would have to move Mr. Thomas to another table. The cot with the new guy was currently parked right in the middle of the room, so she rolled that body out to make room for the transfer. She had been so engrossed in her work that she had no idea how much time had passed. As she glanced at the inaccurate electric clock on the wall, her phone vibrated in her pocket. Was it Johnny? She hoped so, but she really did not have time to look if she were to finish this next embalming in hopes of impressing her dad.

Once she had moved Mr. Thomas aside, she wheeled the cot back into the prep room. She carefully adjusted the table to the height of the cot so she could easily slide this body over with as little effort as possible. As she pulled back the cot cover, she glanced at his tag to find out his name. MERSA the red tag read. Not his name, but a biohazard warning. His name was Clifford J. DuVall. She would have to gear up heavy in protective equipment and double glove. It amazed her that years ago, funeral directors never wore gloves or other personal protection. She was glad that part of the process had evolved. Of course, once AIDS became well-known, most everyone got on the bandwagon. Now every funeral director had to take continuing education about biohazards and communicable disease once per year. Really, a waste of precious time since nothing new was ever taught.

She pulled out a sterile-looking fresh white paper gown from the closet. In the past, her dad had used a lab coat like a doctor's to embalm in, but since all the hype about blood-borne pathogens, her mom refused to do any funeral home laundry in her own machine.

They now had a small set in the basement off the prep room to specifically wash sheets and other needed linens. Even so, her dad now preferred the paper gowns because they had a moisture barrier built into them and sleeves that were elastic around the wrist. She pulled one on then continued with shoe and hair covers and a face mask. She was sure she either looked like a member of the hazmat team, ready to remove nuclear waste, or a surgeon going in for a cancer. She preferred the surgeon look.

"Good afternoon, Mr. DuVall. I will be your surgeon today. No worries, this won't hurt a bit," she joked out loud even though she knew he would not be responding.

Kathleen picked her mix of embalming fluids from the vintage, shiny white cabinet that probably was purchased in the 1950s. Its metal doors with magnetic latches and stainless steel handles still looked brand-new, and the cabinet served its purpose just fine. No one usually came to the prep room, so decor was not a top priority, and if it weren't for its distinct retro style, no one would know it was old. The only new hardware on this piece of equipment was a padlock set that her dad had installed back in the late 1990s because a fad was beginning to take hold where kids were dunking their marijuana joints in formaldehyde for an extreme buzz. Kathleen was too young to have friends involved in drugs at that time, but her dad was afraid some crazed druggy might decide to break in. A creep like that probably would have bashed in the simple metal cabinet anyway.

She carefully filled the machine cylinder with a mix of embalming fluid, anticoagulant, and water then flicked the switch for just a second to blend her mixture. As she returned to the body, she adjusted his head ever so slightly to the right so he would look toward his visitors and crisscrossed his hands over his abdomen to keep his elbows out of the blood as it ran down the table.

Facial orifices were disinfected and features set to create what would hopefully turn out to be a natural-looking expression. She ran her hand along his collarbone to pick just the right area for the incision and ever so precisely dug the cold metal scalpel through the layers of skin and tissue to free the needed circulatory parts. In through the carotid, out through the jugular. With the cannula in place, then clamped tightly to avoid it slipping out of the artery during injection and spraying around the room, she set the pump to start and adjusted the pressure to slow just to be on the safe side. She didn't want to accidently bloat the face. The whir of the machine was like a white noise in a nursery, and it sent a calming buzz through an otherwise disturbing room.

As the blood drained down the table, Kathleen continually massaged the limbs, helping to ensure that the fluid reached all the tissue. She was pleased with her progress, considering that she had only done a few embalmings to date all by herself. At school, there were always lots of students who needed to be present for their required ten preparations to graduate and, of course, the instructors too, so they all took turns.

She was pretty sure Mr. DuVall would need some tissue builder to help push out his sunken cheeks, but that was not something she felt comfortable doing just yet by herself. One wrong move with the needle and a corpse could have irreversible unnatural puffiness. She would leave that job for he dad.

The slurping sound of the embalming machine indicated it was almost out of fluid, and step one would be done. Next, the organ cavities would be thoroughly emptied with a special tool and suction then refilled with an extremely potent wintergreen-scented cavity fluid that burned the nose and throat if you didn't wear a face mask. This was by far the least favorite procedure in preparation as there was no telling what one might suck out of the innards. Finally, a thorough cleaning of the body and Mr. Duvall would be . . . well . . . as good as dead.

Just as the last drop of cavity fluid entered its final resting place, her phone buzzed. She was curious to know who it was and a bit hopeful the text was from Johnny. She decided to quickly finish up with Mr. DuVall first so she would not have to get ungloved. It would only be a few minutes, and if it were Johnny, making him wait a little longer would just build the anticipation she hoped he was feeling.

As she pulled a fresh white sheet over her finished masterpiece, she was glad her day had turned out to be much more productive than she projected. She removed all her personal protective equipment, washed her hands, and then grabbed her phone with an anxious curiosity about the identity of her most recent message sender.

CHAPTER 14

Kathleen was surprised how fast the afternoon had passed. Down in the basement prep room, there was no accurate clock and no windows, so it was difficult to determine what time of day it was. Johnny's text had come in at exactly 5:19 p.m.

It simply read, *"What ya doin'?"*

She was relieved it was informal and took a few more minutes to respond so as not to look overzealous even though it had already been nearly a half hour that had passed.

"Just finished 2 bodies. How bout you?"

"Only body I have thought about today is yours."

She blushed as she read it, then her phone actually rang. Johnny's number appeared on the screen. She answered, trying to not sound too enthusiastic. "Hey, I was just trying to find an appropriate response to your text. What's up?"

"Nothing much, we had a crazy day at the office, and I wanted to hear your voice to take my mind off it. I really don't like texting that much, but everyone else seems to prefer it."

"Well, it is good to hear your voice too," she responded coyly. "My day started out rough, but now I am doing okay."

"Would you like to grab a bite to eat and a cocktail somewhere? I'd really like to vent about my day."

Kathleen realized she had hardly eaten anything all day due to her early morning self-induced puke bug and her afternoon body preparation marathon. Now that he mentioned food, she could feel her stomach growling.

"Yeah, food sounds great, but I will definitely have to pass on the drinks. I had enough last night to keep me away from vodka for a while."

He laughed out loud, surely understanding her choice. "How about I pick you up in about a half hour, we can decide where to eat then?"

She would have to move quickly to shower and look presentable in that short amount of time, but she figured she would just go with an updo to avoid having to blow-dry and curl her hair. She checked in with her father and mother to let them know about her plans to go out.

"You'll have to go to the prep room and check out my work," she informed her father smugly. "I must say, I am pretty good."

"I've already been down, passed you in the front room talking on the phone. And yes, I am quite impressed. An improvement I predict as your way of making up from last night's behavior."

He smirked as he spoke to be sure she knew he was not angry about her lack of commitment to her duties. After all, she had just returned home from college and had years ahead to be stuck at the funeral home, waiting for the next call. He had done many calls alone before and knew she would fall into a routine once the newness of being home wore off. "Go out and have a good time, but not too good, since tomorrow will be a long day." He went on to explain, "We will have calling hours one to three and funeral service beginning at three o'clock for Mr. Thomas. The DuVall family will be in at ten o'clock for arrangements, which won't leave us much time before the Thomas family arrives. We are going to have a busy day."

Her Mom was cooking something that smelled delicious, probably pasta she gathered, by the scent of basil and oregano permeating the air, and Kathleen almost regretted not checking on what was for dinner before deciding to go out. She loved her mom's cooking and had not had time for very many home-cooked meals yet. "Would you make some chicken divine for me tomorrow, Mom?" she inquired.

"Sure, honey, it's been a while since I've made that. Plus, we would love to have you home for dinner. It's been a whirlwind for all of us since you arrived home," her mother commented caringly.

She admired her mom's commitment to her duties as a wife and mother, giving up any dreams of her own to be a dedicated funeral director's wife. She was pretty sure her mom was happy with her life, but they had never really talked about it. Even if she wasn't, there would have been no way to tell. She always smiled and always took very good care of her family.

Kathleen finally moved along quickly, having wasted nearly ten minutes talking with her mom and dad. She cut her shower short and skipped shaving her legs to give her an excuse to ward off any sexual advances she might be tempted to accept. She needed to make it home early so that perhaps she could sit in on the arrangements for Mr. DuVall in the morning. She absolutely needed to get more experience with the paperwork and other arrangement duties as those things were not covered in school. That was why the residency was a year long, to ensure one could embalm and have opportunity to learn the business side of funeral directing as well.

Kathleen chose her favorite pair of jeans and a bright-pink sweater. Although black was slimming, it was the last color she would wear off duty. Just a little makeup, thanks to inheriting her dad's great complexion, and a quick clip in her long red hair would suffice. She had turned to walk downstairs when she heard the doorbell. She was glad he had the decency to come to the door rather than just honk. Her dad would be more receptive to her leaving with a man who had that much dignity. Wow, she just said *man*. It amazed her that she and Johnny were actually grown-ups now, with real jobs and big-people responsibilities. It was an exciting time.

She could hear her her mom and dad making small talk with Johnny, her dad commenting on his new position at the coroner's office. "Listen, son, whatever you do, don't let it go to your head. We need more men like old Joe in that office. Some of those younger ones are a little cocky."

"No, sir, I am eager to learn the business and help out any way I can in this community. I have pride in my hometown and respect for people who work in it."

Johnny knew exactly what Mr. DelGiorno was talking about. So many of the guys wouldn't "get their hands dirty" to help at a scene. They wanted to be the big man who pronounced the death then stand idly by, watching others work. Johnny was hoping that he could change that image a little and perhaps earn a higher spot doing more work directly with the ME. The whole autopsy process was intriguing to him. He had considered going back to college but was not keen on attending school another six years and going into debt up to his ass. Now that he had a foot in the door as a part-time coroner, he could turn on his charm, work hard, and hopefully become an ME's assistant. Good pay, no college debt, and close enough to the action to appease him.

As Kathleen entered the room, Johnny's eyes tried unsuccessfully to not show his desire for her. It was surely obvious to everyone in the room. Kathleen smiled approvingly as she too was eager to see him, even though she sort of wished she hadn't been promiscuous so soon. It wasn't like they had just met or something though, and she hoped that would mean something to him to avoid her coming off as a sleaze. She was really feeling her hunger pains, so she kept the conversation moving toward the door as she walked through the kitchen, grabbing her coat and heading to the exit.

"I won't be late," she commented to let her parents know but to also remind herself to get in at a decent hour. "Call if you need me, really." Even though she hoped he wouldn't so she could spend more time with Johnny.

CHAPTER 15

They decided on a local pizzeria, mainly because Kathleen was so famished she didn't want to wait for a server and cook to get her food at a sit-down restaurant. The old-time Italian owners still made the dough fresh daily, and she was craving a sub made with their fresh-baked rolls. The combination of the soft bread, mayo, and ham with all the fixins' was making her mouth water just thinking about it.

Johnny was a pizza guy and ordered a few different specialty slices. It was amazing how the workers there never wrote an order down, and although it was not a huge place, they would walk your food right to your table just a few minutes following your order. One must have had to prove photographic memory to be hired there. Kathleen could barely remember a thing without a list, so even as a kid, when she had looked for a summer job, she did not even apply there. She had ended up working as a cashier at the local Mobil station until she had left for college, then waitressed a few nights in Syracuse while in mortuary school. Her dad took good care of her financially, but she still liked to contribute. She liked having a little money to herself without having to feel guilty about every purchase she made.

Dinner came speedily, and Kathleen quickly dug in. She had hoped that Johnny didn't think she was a pig, but she was starved. She could tell that something was bothering Johnny and prayed that it was not regret about their encounter last evening.

"So what time did you leave last night? I had no recollection of your departure when I finally came to this morning."

"Gosh, it must have been around ten o'clock or so. You shooed me out, worried your parents would be home soon."

"Dad got a call last night, and I missed helping due to my condition. Luckily he was not too mad. Anyway, I tried to make it up today in body preparation. By the way, did we get all our clothing out of the hearse last night?" She could tell her face was becoming red. "I would be humiliated if my dad were to have found any evidence."

"Oh, Jesus!" he shouted as he raised his hand to his mouth. "I couldn't find my underwear this morning," he sarcastically commented.

Her red face was now burning up. And they both burst out in laughter.

"Johnny Pietrobini, you are an ass!"

As she watched him, she was so glad that fate had brought them together. The death of another had turned into a good thing for her. How morbid, she thought. "You mentioned that you had a tough day at work?" she questioned. "Is it something you would like to talk about?"

He appreciated her thoughtfulness. He also appreciated that she knew a lot about the business so he could probably discuss things with her that he could not tell others. Some would think it too gloomy, others just too gross.

"Well, I don't have a lot of details yet, and you have to swear not to tell anyone, because I am trying to work my way up the ladder at the coroner's office"

"I promise you can trust me. Besides, I will have stories to vent about sometimes, and I will need a confidant."

The word sounded a bit committing, but she thought that if things worked out between them, they might make a good couple because they could talk about odd things that happened in their work. She felt quite flattered that he was considering confiding in her about that part of his life so quickly. It reassured her she was wrong in thinking that he might have regretted last evening or thought less of her because of it.

"We've got a strange case at the office," he began. "The family of one of the patients at Clear Rivers had requested an autopsy a couple of months back. Unusual because in the nursing homes, there is no reason to do them, but the family insisted. As it turns out, the patient was poisoned. They are thinking maybe a nurse or doctor, but the investigation will take a while." He went on somewhat hesitant but clearly needing someone to discuss it with. "I could probably lose my job for even mentioning this, because it is under investigation, but boy, did it knock the wind out of my sails today. Imagine, there is possibly a murderer walking around our lovely small town?"

He told her about the newest policies that required them to collect blood samples from any hospital, home, or nursing facility death until they could find more answers. This meant that even with hospice calls, which were expected deaths, the coroner would need to come out to do the draw before releasing the body. This meant more chances for him to be called out and lots more work to do. It also meant more holdups for the funeral homes, but Kath would have to deal with the inconveniences, and besides, perhaps she would run into Johnny more at work too. That would be worth the hassle.

The rest of dinner was somewhat quiet. How could they top that conversation? But even in the silence, Kathleen enjoyed being with Johnny. As he excused himself from the table to refill his soda, she was surprised she had never taken notice of his cute butt and charming personality. It was probably okay they hadn't hooked up as teenagers because those relationships rarely lasted long anyway. Perhaps they would hate each other now if they had. Their progression in years at least offered a maturity that might allow for this relationship to go somewhere. Either way, she planned to have fun with him and enjoy whatever path they went on for now.

With a full stomach, Kathleen began to feel sleepy. "I probably should get home. I am in for a long day tomorrow. Mom is making a great homemade meal around six, would you like to join us?"

He nodded as he began to inch out of the booth. "I couldn't think of anyone better to have dinner with, again."

He grabbed her hand as they headed for the door, and the comfort of her hand in his made his day improve tenfold.

CHAPTER 16

It was going to be a busy day, arrangements and calling hours leading into a church funeral. Between setting up a body and flowers and getting all the paperwork and other preparation done on the second call, the day would not be short of things to do. Mr. DelGiorno was already in the funeral home when Kathleen got up even though she had thought that she was way ahead of the game. "Dad, what would you like me to do first?"

"Well, flowers are already starting to arrive, so let's get Mr. Thomas casketed and on the bier so we can set flowers before we get overwhelmed with them. I have a feeling this will be a pretty big call due to his popularity in the community."

Although not recently, Mr. Thomas had belonged to many organizations in the community and had even been mayor in their town for a while many years ago. Mr. DelGiorno had buried Mr. Thomas's wife nearly fifteen years ago, and they had been very close ever since. In a rare occurrence, Jules and Kathleen happened to be out of town that evening for a shopping trip and would be home late. When the calling hours were over for Mrs. Thomas, Steve had gone outdoors to put out the trash. When he returned, he found he was locked out of both the funeral home and house. Steve noticed Mr. Thomas's lights were on, and he still had family visiting, so he thought, what the heck, perhaps he could hang out there until his wife returned to unlock the door.

As awkward as he had felt knocking on their door, they welcomed him in with open arms, laughed about his situation, and he played poker for hours with Mr. Thomas and his sons. Ever since then, there was an open invitation for Steve to join his card group to play poker or euchre every Friday night when he did not have a funeral call. He was going to miss Mr. Thomas dearly. Even though they were years apart in age, Steve always appreciated his friendship and did many things to help Mr. Thomas out when his own sons weren't available. He had become like a second father to Steve, since his own dad had passed years ago.

As they began to move Mr. Thomas from the table to the casket, Kathleen on the feet because it was the lighter end, her dad began to get teary-eyed. As they lay him comfortably in the casket, Kathleen pretended she needed to grab something in the other room to give her dad a moment to compose. She could hear him crying ever so slightly from the other room and knew this would be a tough day for Dad.

Mr. DelGiorno was appreciative of her disappearance, as he was not the type to get attached to people often. It was too hard in this business, but he was attached to Mr. Thomas, and he unselfishly grieved today for himself for a change.

When she thought she had given him enough time, she returned to help her dad move the casket upstairs. Kathleen and her dad put the final touches on the viewing room, lit the candles at either end of the casket, and placed the kneeler in front for prayers. Mr. DelGiorno expected the family early, as usual. They would need some time to get settled and grieve before other callers arrived. Mr. DelGiorno hoped that his own earlier breakdown would have been enough to allow him to keep it together once the family arrived. He didn't want to look weak to the family or Kathleen.

As they waited at the door, twice in conversation, Kath had almost spilled the beans about the poisonings in town, but she knew that she couldn't breathe a word of it. He would probably gather that something was up once the coroner started showing up on all home deaths, even those under a physician's care. She wasn't going to be the one to let the cat out of the bag and risk the chance of losing Johnny's trust.

Out of the front window in the door, they could see the family begin to walk over from their father's house next door. A sense of dread and relief overcame Mr. DelGiorno. He was anxious to get the family there so that the initial viewing and approval would be over, but he just wasn't sure if he would be overcome with sadness, especially once the family began to cry. They came in a large group. Both of his sons, their wives, and all their children and spouses must have equaled at least sixteen people. Nearly everyone was dressed in black, all neat, tidy, and ready for the day's events. Each carefully signed their name in the guest book at the door and took a memorial card with the prayer they had chosen and Mr. Thomas's name and dates of birth and death: January 1, 1927–June 1, 2011.

Mr. DelGiorno guided them through to the viewing room, even though they had been there enough over the years to know where to go. He watched as they approached the casket and was surprised that they chatted and shook their heads instead of the typical convergence to the kneeler for prayers. *What is wrong?* He began thinking of a number of possibilities. *Cosmetics too heavy, hair not parted right, worse was he leaking somewhere?*

Dave, Mr. Thomas's oldest son approached Mr. DelGiorno. "We're a little confused, because that is not the suit we brought in for Dad."

Along with a surge of adrenaline, hundreds of thoughts began pouring through Mr. DelGiorno's head. *How could this be?* He remembered another time, when the daughter of a deceased kept screaming from the front room, "That's not my mother!" but as it turned out, that was just her grief crying in denial that she had actually passed. Or the time Mrs. Perry's grandson had stopped by to view her before leaving town and returned promptly from the viewing room to inform Mr. DelGiorno that that was *not* his grandmother. Luckily, the true confusion was that Mrs. Perry's viewing was set for the next day, so she was still in the prep room because Mrs. Wood was currently being shown. Disaster averted.

But this had never happened. They must be mistaken. There was no way. It must be a momentary lapse of reason due to grief. *Shit!* It all suddenly became clear as he recalled that Kathleen had dressed Mr. Thomas yesterday when he met with the next family. The clothing for both bodies would have been in the prep room, and both clients were about the same size. Being used to working alone, it had never occurred to him to label the clothing—it wasn't necessary. Kathleen's newness just didn't provide her with the insight to make sure she checked with her dad about which was which. He turned to Kathleen with a look of horror, and she knew right away something was up. He was actually more pissed at himself for not having noticed when they casketed him, but he had been busy and somewhat distracted. "Why don't you move into the north viewing room, while Kathleen and I take care of this? I am very sorry, we have two calls, and there must have been a mix-up with the clothing. It will be brief. We just need a few minutes."

He spoke with a calmness that would make one believe his insides were not churning with fury. He grabbed Kathleen's arm and quietly informed her of the mix-up and instructed her to go get the right clothes from the prep room.

She could feel the sense of panic flow through her cheeks and down to her gut as she realized her prompt work making up for her previous bad behaviors had turned out to be a disaster. "But, Dad, I just dressed Mr. DuVall this morning. It will take me a few minutes."

"Move, girl," he demanded. "I will keep them occupied and have Mom fix them some coffee. As soon as you get back with the clothing, shut the doors, and I'll meet you in there."

She moved like she never had, and Mr. Duvall was stripped of most of his attire in no time. She was thankful that she had decided to cut the suit coat and shirt up the back for ease of dressing. Often her dad would take the time to put the clothing on without altering it, but thankfully, she hadn't mastered that trade yet.

She entered the viewing room, closed both doors for privacy, and began working on what she could without help, moving some of the flowers, the kneeler and candles so they could open the bottom end of the casket and have better access. Nothing like undoing a lot of work. It wasn't long before her dad entered too, and they set out to fix the mistake together.

They worked diligently but silently. Neither daring to say a word. Mr. DelGiorno for fear of exploding in anger and Kathleen for fear of bursting into tears. As they shimmied off his trousers, both were mortified at the discovery of the leopard thong. That should have tipped Kathleen off when she was dressing him, perhaps. How stupid, she thought. Another lesson from the field: never dress a body without confirming the clothes belong to the deceased.

Dressing a body was bad enough on a prep table, but undressing and redressing a body that was already in a casket was a complete nightmare. There was no way those thongs were coming off, and besides, would it be right to put them on Mr. DuVall now anyway? This secret had to go straight to the grave with Mr. Thomas, and it would.

Once again they went through the process of resetting all the equipment. Flowers, candles, and kneeler placed just so. Although in a hurry, they still ensured everything on and in the casket was straight and presentable. As they placed the last bouquet of flowers on the display stand, Mr. DelGiorno made one last adjustment to the casket throw, and they were finally satisfied they could allow the family to return.

By the time they were finished, Mr. DelGiorno rightfully was drenched in sweat. Thankfully, his suit coat would cover the pit stains that had accumulated. He grabbed for his hankie in his back left pocket, wiped his brow, straightened his tie, then left to get the family without ever saying a word to Kathleen.

Calling hours dragged on, and the silent treatment nearly drove Kathleen nuts. She wondered if he would have been less upset if it hadn't been Mr. Thomas. She wondered if he would be mad for a long time. Not likely though, as he was a reasonable man and usually didn't hold a grudge, especially with her. Still, it had already been a while, and he hadn't seemed to ease up. Perhaps he stayed angry at her to keep him from crying for Mr. Thomas. That seemed logical. She kept thinking, hoping rather, that they would laugh about this someday, just as everyone had been so delighted by the story he told during her graduation dinner about his own father being mortified by something he had done wrong.

The funeral service at the Episcopal Church was a new experience for Kathleen. The church was elaborate with beautifully colored stained glass windows and high arching ceilings. Much like the Catholic Church, she often wondered why it was necessary to go to such expense just to worship God but still admired its beauty and distinct architecture. God would not think that necessary, would He? She couldn't help but to think how wasteful it was since people struggled to have shelter and food in this world.

The service for Mr. Thomas was quite short, actually very short, she guessed, but never having been to an Episcopal service, she really didn't know for sure. He father confirmed her suspicion as they returned to the hearse. "Hate those bastards," he ranted, "Mr. Thomas deserved a respectful service just as every other congregant does. He gave a lot of money to this church, and just because his Father was out of town and the family requested the service late in the day that is no excuse to cut his service short!"

Kathleen knew her dad was angry for sure because he rarely said curse words, especially words directed at a man of the cloth. She agreed with her father about the service but couldn't help but wonder if some of his anger was also directed toward her mistake from today. Or maybe it was his way of getting over his anger at her by turning it over to someone else. Either way, she agreed with her dad. It was evident that churches were becoming more and more like businesses instead of places of worship. It seemed that no one really dedicated their lives to serving God and His parishioners like they did years ago. She had seen many of these same changes in her own church over the years.

It was happening in every church though. Just recently, a family had requested a pastor from the local "cult" church. Kathleen called it that because it was a church that had grown so big over the last couple years it was almost a farce. New buildings went up like hotels in Vegas. Elaborate in such a way that it almost screamed Jim and Tammy Faye Baker. Was this really what God envisioned? She often thought.

Anyway, this family was denied the courtesy of a pastor to do a short funeral service for their relative who was not a member of the church but had attended occasionally with other family members who belonged. After getting through to the main office and being transferred to several other important people, it was confirmed that, indeed, they could not possibly spare one of their three pastors on Thursday for a short service in the funeral home because they had a wedding in the church that Saturday. In other words—sorry buddy, you apparently had not provided enough money to our church for us to even consider saying a fifteen-minute blessing over your grave. Now that wasn't what one expects from an organization who claims to be dedicated to serving God and His people. Kathleen's dad was furious then too.

As they finished Mr. Thomas's services at the cemetery, which was also very brief, the family shook hands and hugged the DelGiornos and extended an invite to the reception they were holding at the local Moose Lodge. Mr. DelGiorno graciously had to decline the invitation, making an excuse that they had dinner company coming tonight. This actually was true, because Kathleen had invited Johnny to join them tonight, although Mr. DelGiorno was unaware. Kathleen was surprised he had declined but realized he was physically and mentally exhausted from the day's events and the death of his close friend. The stress showed today on his face like never before. His usual sparkle was just not there today, even with the early June sun reflecting on him.

Slowly each family member began to move toward their cars. As the family pulled away and the final car turned the last corner before disappearing into the world beyond the cemetery gates, Mr.

DelGiorno grabbed a handful of dirt, thoughtfully tossed it on the casket, and began sobbing for his loss. He didn't stop until the casket was lowered and the lid was securely sealed on the vault.

CHAPTER 17

"Delgiorno Funeral Home, this is Kathleen speaking."
She almost trembled in fear because she realized that this would be the first time she had answered a death call, if this actually happened to be one. Weeks had passed, and the funeral home had been pretty slow. Their last two calls had been direct cremation with no services, so she actually was hoping this might be the call to break the boredom.

Kathleen gathered the usual information from the family and inquired about a convenient time for them to come in to make arrangements. "Dad," she hollered through the funeral home as she finished her call, "we have a death call at St. James in Elmira. Why don't I go ahead and make the removal? The family plans to be here in about an hour."

She had made enough mistakes in her first weeks working at the funeral home to last a lifetime, but finally, she felt that her dad had forgiven her and still trusted her. There was no way that they could be sure to get back in time to meet the family if both went on the removal, and Kathleen knew that she still hadn't had enough practice with arrangement. Anyway, she was not allowed to sign a contract until she became officially licensed through the state following her residency.

"Are you sure you know where to go alone? I can call Roger to see if he can help out."

"That's silly, I am sure I can take care of it alone. Let me make you proud," she sarcastically responded. She looked at this as an opportunity to show she could do the work. Plus, Roger lived at least thirty minutes away in the opposite direction of the hospital and she wanted to get home in time to see Johnny.

"Call me if you run into any problems, and don't forget to check the tag before you remove. They often have two or three in the cooler. Clothes are one thing, but mix up a body, and we'll have a lawsuit." He smirked jokingly as he commented, although Kathleen knew there was some real seriousness to what he had said.

As Kathleen was preparing to go on her first solo removal at a hospital, she ran over in her mind twice all the things she would need to do to make sure she got it right. Sign in at reception, back to the car for the cot, enter through the back, and then down to the basement morgue. She had been there just once with her dad but was confident that she could do this alone. Every day that passed, she gained new insight and self-assurance in her ability to get it right; it was becoming second nature for her.

She pulled away in the hearse, unaware of her dad watching through the office window. He couldn't believe that his next generation was beginning to take over. He thought back to her youth. When she was very little, they tried hard to keep her sheltered from the funeral home. Kids, death, nightmares, it had just seemed like the right thing to do. He laughed as he remembered the year that he had seriously considered buying a truck. Part of an early midlife crisis, must be, as it was common for all funeral directors to drive a Cadillac or Lincoln, no real reason he guessed, just the way it was.

It wasn't like they needed a second car or really could afford one at that time, but Jules and he had discussed it several times, apparently in front of Kathleen. Back then, they still rented hearses from other local homes because it was quite expensive to own one outright, and with a four-year-old daughter, money was swiftly allocated to many other necessities. Steve had just finished a call and decided to ask Kathleen to ride along to return the hearse to the neighboring town. He figured a little company would be good, and Jules would appreciate the break.

As Kathleen bounded out of the house to pile in the car, she hesitated briefly and shouted in delight toward the pristine Cadillac hearse, "Is this your new truck, Daddy?"

He didn't have the heart to tell her what the car was actually used for, but simply said no, it was just a friend's truck. It wasn't long after that incident that it became too hard to hide the secrets of death and funerals from an inquisitive child. She gradually became aware and involved in what went on in the other side of their house, and it never seemed to bother her one bit. She was a natural. In fact, he recalled she preferred to play house and dolls over at the funeral home because, as she touted, "The furniture is much more fanciest, and I am going to be rich, so I will need to play over here!"

He sort of understood why it never bothered her. Just as death hadn't bothered him at first because in most cases, the person lying in wake was not someone he knew. If you had never seen the living side of a person, walking, talking, and carrying on with life, it was easy to accept they never did live. It was a distance, even a wall, perhaps, which kept those exposed to death every day sane. Yet the longer one stayed in the business, sooner or later, the people that were once easy to disconnect with because you had never known as living became fewer and fewer. It became a bit harder to shield oneself from the inevitable that even you and every loved one you cherish would be lying there someday.

Steven hoped it would be a long time before Kathleen experienced his depth of knowing everyone that she buried, but it was not likely going to happen. She had grown up in Watkins Glen, and she would have connections in one way or another to most clients of DelGiorno Funeral Home. She would be fine, he reassured himself. She had been going to church more often, and that would bring her some comfort, he thought. They would also have each other to lean on when needed, although now that she was there and could do so much around the home, the idea of retirement kept creeping back into his mind more and more often.

The ringing doorbell pulled Mr. DelGiorno back to the business at hand. The family was several minutes early, and his recent descent down memory lane had prohibited him from being ready with all the paperwork and price lists he needed for arrangements. He hurried to gather what he needed and placed it on the arrangement desk before he greeted the family at the door. "You must be the Anderson family. I am terribly sorry for your loss."

"No big deal, we really couldn't stand him anyway, the miserable old bat. Now don't try to sell us some fancy casket and service," she continued, "we want the basics, and that is it."

Steven wondered how this lady had room to be discussing how miserable someone might have been, given her lovely demeanor. He could tell right away this was a woman not to be reckoned with. Her skin was wrinkled much too early for her age, which Steven calculated based on Mr. Anderson's age and the fact that she must be his daughter. Even if he had had her at the age of seventeen, she could be at the most sixty. She smelled of old cigarettes, and he was certain she was a smoker due to the fact that her once obviously white hair was yellowed not from a dye but nicotine. He peeked out and noticed she had arrived in an old Ford pickup, which had more rust on it than he had ever believed could be present without a vehicle being in the scrapyard. Mounds of hay were in the back, which revealed to him that the other scent he was still trying to figure out must have been farm manure. "Why don't we go ahead and have a seat in the office and we will discuss all the details there."

He was glad it would be him dealing with this prize instead of Kathleen, as they would have surely clashed in the personality department. "Fine, but don't think by putting me in some fancy office that I will change my mind. I am not falling for you sales tricks."

He wondered what "sales tricks" she was referring to. Perhaps she thought she had just entered a car dealership, but he loved the challenge. While he would never sell a family something they did not need or want, he always managed to get families to warm up to him by the end of arrangements once they realized his intentions were good. He enjoyed that part of the business and prided himself for being compassionate. He certainly did not want a family to buy things they might later regret and then, worse, not pay for either.

It was not uncommon for families to come in angry; after all, the funeral director was often the first person they saw after death, many times someone they don't know, and damn it, often they were pissed, so why not take it out on the funeral director? Steven, however, had an uncanny way of getting people to relax. His job was to direct them through the process, help them make difficult decisions, and guide them to the closure they needed to heal. Once people saw this side of him, they usually warmed up, but he questioned whether he would crack this nut. "It is going to be a cremation. How much will that be? I don't want to spend much, because he never spent a dime on anyone else."

"No problem, ma'am, we can take care of that service. Can we start with your relationship to Mr. Anderson?" He continued, "We usually start by gathering personal information for the deceased, then we will move into the details of the service."

"There ain't goin' to be no services, but suit yourself. I am his daughter, although I don't tell many people that. I am only here because my brother and sister live out of town. What else do you need? This place gives me the damn creeps."

Oh, crack this nut indeed he would not. He wanted her to be out just as much as she did. He made record time filling out the obituary record and death certificate information and didn't even discuss with her some of the options available for cremation services, like memorial cards and urns. Just as he was wrapping up, she had one final question. "What about the cat? He has a cat we would like to have put with him, can we do that?"

"Sure, just bring it with you to the burial."

Although they chose direct cremation, Mr. Anderson was still to be buried on the plot with his wife. It wasn't uncommon for people to have their pets cremated when the pet died then save the cremains to be buried with them. It actually was a comfort for many to know their pets would remain with them, and Mr. DelGiorno was happy to accommodate that.

"Good, may I use your phone?"

"Yes, it is right here, help yourself." He confirmed as he lifted the old black receiver off the base and turned the rotary dial toward her. Although they had a cordless phone too, he had never switched out that old phone for nostalgic reasons. He remembered the day his grandfather had it installed back when Bell telephone still charged to rent phones because they weren't yet available in department stores. It was too important to give up, even if it was cumbersome.

She dialed carefully, clearly annoyed at the inconvenience of having to actually dial a phone. He guessed the cheap old biddy probably didn't have touch-tone phones in her own home either, if she even had a phone.

A surge of appall overtook Mr. DelGiorno as he listened to the one-sided conversation she had.

"Yeah, Henry, it's Mom." She paused briefly to make sure he understood who it was then simply said, "Shoot the cat."

Just a short while later, Henry promptly delivered the cat in a garbage bag for burial with its owner.

CHAPTER 18

Kath pulled into the back entrance of the hospital and carefully backed the hearse up to the loading ramp. So carefully had any onlookers been watching, they would have guessed she was ninety years old. She had never been good at backing up, but when you added the length of the hearse and the view-inhibiting curtains in the rear windows to the mix, it made backing up a dreadful task.

Before she even got out of the car, she once again went through the checklist in her mind. She wanted to be swift because she hoped to be home before it got dark. It was a little inconvenient that funeral directors had to park in the back and walk all the way through the back end of the hospital to the main elevators, which were in the front of the hospital, then go to the second-floor registrar to sign for the body and collect the death certificate and morgue key. Then walk all the way back through the hospital to the hearse to get the cot, travel back through a different set of windy hallways, and descend to the basement morgue on the service elevator to collect the body.

After the body was loaded, she had to return to the registrar to take back the morgue key. Just to get to the body usually took about a half hour, and that was if there was no line when she made it to the registrar.

She contemplated the silly procedure, but apparently it would be wrong to park the hearse at the front circle of the hospital to first collect the paperwork then drive out back. For Christ's sake, someone might then know that people die at the hospital.

It took her the usual half hour, but she was glad she could at least text while she made the walk from the car and back. It kept her busy, so the time seemed to pass quicker. She made contact with Johnny, and they agreed to meet later, which made her work even faster so that she could catch up with him sooner.

As she arrived back at the hearse, she was careful to release the legs on the cot at just the right moment so it did not hit the ground. Off to a good start, she thought as she pushed the cot up the ramp and buzzed the buzzer to get in again. Her dad had a pass card, but she forgot to grab it. It reminded her that she should ask the registrar about one for herself when she returned the morgue key. She wondered why they didn't install a pass card system on the morgue door too. That would save a lot of walking for the poor funeral director.

She proceeded down the service elevator to the dingy yellow hallway that led to the morgue. This elevator was a little more modern than the healthcare facility in Watkins; at least the doors closed on their own, so the concern of losing a finger was minimal. She remembered there would be quite a bit of room in the morgue because this hospital also performed autopsies in the same room, so maneuvering the cot would be a little easier for her. As she went to slip the key in the door, she noticed it was already opened slightly. *Didn't need this damn key that I now have to take the time to return,* she thought, quite annoyed.

As she entered, the curtain between the cooler and other room was pulled. As she peeked around, there were several staff members doing an autopsy, and she could see the medical examiner with hands up to his elbows in a man's torso. She turned quickly around and set about her work, not especially enjoying what she had just seen. As she pulled back the first cooler door, she could see they were full.

She checked the toe tags carefully, and sure enough, her body was on the bottom shelf. Her mind raced. *How the hell I am going to get this damn body two and a half feet off the ground to get it on the cot?* She knew the cot could be lowered to the ground and the man slid over, but she wasn't sure she would be able to lift it back up alone.

There was no way she was calling her dad. She had given him enough grief the past few months, and this removal was a way to show him she could get things done right. She stood there dumbfounded for more than a few minutes. Maybe she would text Johnny and see if he would come? Not very logical, as it would take him at least thirty minutes to get there. "Excuse me," she said to the ME behind the curtain as she cleared her throat. "Would it be possible for someone to give me a quick hand over here?"

"Call for an orderly, that is not our job," the ME called back to her condescendingly.

Prick! Her dad was right, she quickly realized. "Must be all coroners and ME's are egotistical asses," she whispered to herself. *Fine,* she thought. *I will just have to take my chances and figure this out. If I still can't do it, I'll call an orderly.* She'd find out from Johnny who this jerk was and be sure he gave it back to him whenever he could. She took a mental note of any features that might identify who he was. Maybe she could find a glass eye for Johnny to drop in his coffee at the office.

Just as she dropped the legs on the head end of the cot, a face popped in the door. Relief set in a bit. It was Pete, a local director in Elmira whom she had met a few times because the firm where he worked was also where DelGiorno Funeral Home took their bodies for cremation. She had often picked up cremains for her father when she was home summers from college and knew him from those visits.

By the look on her face, Pete knew right away that Kathleen needed some help, and he was willing to jump right in. She hadn't been happier to see someone since she went to her first Aerosmith concert in 2002 during the Girls of Summer Tour and got to meet her heartthrob, Steve Tyler. In fact right now, she would have given up that experience just to have someone help her.

"I'll give you a hand here, then you can give me a hand, and we will both be out of here quicker," he suggested in a rather helpful-sounding voice.

"That would be great!"

Pete showed Kathleen how to bring the cot back up one end at a time without dropping a body off it. More experience she could never get in a classroom, only on the job.

"Thank God there are good people that are still modest enough to help others out!" she said purposefully and quite loud as they left the morgue.

Pete even offered to return the key to the registrar, saving Kath more time.

By now, she had probably been gone for close to two hours and still had a half-hour drive before she would be back home. She almost wished this call was a cremation so that there would be no embalming when she returned. They had been having lots of cremations lately, but her dad preferred the old-fashioned, traditional services with hours and funeral. She knew that those services provided more income, and with two people now on the payroll, she felt a little guilty wishing for a cremation.

As she opened the hospital door, it was already dusk. She hurried along so that she would be out of the way for Pete to back his hearse up when he emerged with his corpse. All loaded, she headed for the highway and flicked on some tunes to make the long drive seem a little shorter.

She was plugging right along on the highway, not really paying close attention to her speed. Out of the corner of her eye, she saw a light flash in the rearview mirror. She glanced at her speedometer, seventy-seven! *Shit, am I being pulled over?* She glanced back to check her rearview again, but instead of police lights, she was mesmerized by a vision of her sixth-grade teacher, Mrs. Updike. She had been her first teacher in public school. Her dad had mentioned that he had met with her several weeks ago to make her prearrangement. She had called him to meet with her right at the hospital.

Kathleen was freaked out a little, but this vision brought more of a sense of peace than fright, as the last two visions had. Still, why did she keep seeing faces appear in the rearview mirror? She was sure hoping that this would stop. No doubt she'd be committed soon if it didn't.

As quickly as the image appeared, it disappeared, and she used only her side mirrors the rest of the way home just to be safe. When she arrived home, Dad offered to do the embalming, and she had had enough for the day, so she gratefully accepted his offer. Then she left promptly to meet Johnny.

Kathleen was relieved the next morning when she awoke to find that Mrs. Updike did not die in the night and thought perhaps her curse was ending. She thought about telling her dad or Johnny about the visions but then thought better of it. They would certainly think she was off her rocker. Instead, she grabbed some sunblock and a towel and then headed to the lakefront to clear her head.

CHAPTER 19

Mr. DelGiorno glanced at the newspaper obituaries to see what the competition was doing. He and Kathleen had been quite busy lately, and he was hoping that it would stay that way. Having someone to share the workload was relieving for him, and he and Jules had been able to enjoy each other quite a bit more lately. They even had been going out more, including visits to many of the restaurants and wineries around both Keuka and Seneca Lakes, a luxury they had not been able to enjoy much before. He could tell that it meant a lot to Jules, and he wanted her to be happy.

As he registered the date listed on the paper, he could hardly believe that three months had passed since Kathleen graduated. She was picking up the trade rather quickly. She had been making most of the prearrangements with families and even had done everything but sign the contract on a few at-need arrangements too. Mr. DelGiorno knew that prearrangements would help ensure Kathleen enjoyed a lucrative business after his retirement.

Kathleen was getting pretty serious with Johnny, and although Mr. DelGiorno had envisioned her with a funeral director, he liked Johnny a lot, and his job was conducive with a funeral director's life. He had recently been promoted to ME assistant full-time as he had hoped and had been able to leave his job at the fire station. Both jobs were under the same state retirement system, so he was able to transfer his retirement and service credits for seniority. This was working out well for him, and it assured Mr. DelGiorno that he was a hard worker, unlike many of the other people in that office. If not, Johnny wouldn't have been promoted so quickly. He also was already helping out a little at the funeral home during their busy times and seemed to enjoy that too. Maybe only because he got to spend time with Kathleen, but maybe he truly did like the work.

The phone rang, but Steve didn't jump up because after only one ring, it stopped. He figured that Kathleen must have gotten it and went about reading his paper. A few moments later, he heard Kathleen entering the room. "Dad, it's the VA. There is a soldier who has been killed in Iraq, and we will be handling the call. It sounds pretty complicated. Can you pick up? I just don't want to mess anything up."

"Sure, honey, what is the name of your contact person?"

"Lieutenant Sergeant Myers," she replied as she handed him the second cordless phone.

The details were indeed complicated. So many things had to happen between Iraq, his home base in Fort Bragg, North Carolina, and then his final destination of Watkins Glen, New York. His body would never be without at least one soldier guard, right up to the burial. Mr. DelGiorno would suggest the National Cemetery, as he was always stunned by its beauty since the day his fifth-grade class had placed flags on each grave in the cemetery for Memorial Day, which was still a traditional fifth-grade field trip. The white headstones all perfectly matched and organized in tidy rows and columns were visually breathtaking. Although the cemetery represented death, it represented so much more. It symbolized all those who had sacrificed for American freedom, whether they had died in active duty or not.

Mr. DelGiorno had decided it would be best for him to make the trip to meet the plane with Staff Sergeant Tony Rusitani's body. He would also have to transport the attending soldier in the hearse too. They often had the hearse pull right onto the runway to load the casket right as the military jet landed. He needed to take care of this himself. It brought back memories of Vietnam. Mr. DelGiorno was lucky to never have been drafted, but many of his friends were and many never came home alive. It was his way of showing respect to all soldiers who died in active duty. He wanted no stone unturned, no mistakes, everything to be as perfect as possible for this call.

This soldier was four years younger than Kathleen, just a baby, really. They were supposed to be out of Iraq by now, but President Obama kept pussyfooting around with withdraw of troops, and now another soldier was dead. Not just a soldier, but one who was just embarking on life itself. He had recently been married and was on his second tour of duty because his commitment to his country and fellow soldiers was so strong he had reenlisted. They had married just before his second deployment so that she could move to the base and at least see him for the short time he was going to be home. He had been stationed there for sixty-four days exactly. A roadside bomb took out a tanker he was riding in, and he was killed by shrapnel.

At both the removal and services, the young soldiers who attended his casket were babies themselves. It was almost humorous how polished and grown-up they looked in their uniforms yet so clearly obvious how much they truly did not know about this world. They asked a lot of questions of Mr. DelGiorno and needed help to drape the flag properly. It made sense though. Mr. DelGiorno did this every day, and many of these boys had never even been to a funeral. Yet here they were, burying a platoon mate, and in charge of making sure he was buried properly. It was also very ironic to Mr. DelGiorno that the Purple Heart he had to place inside the casket was one of the most-honored medals, yet many soldiers never got to see their own. Mr. DelGiorno was glad to help the young men and felt comforted that even though there was nothing he could do to help Staff

Sergeant Rusitani, he was making a difference for these boys. It was kind of like an unspoken trade-off, you give to me my freedom; I'll give you anything I can.

The only comforting part of the entire service was that Tony came home in one piece, and his family would be able to see his face and hold his hands one more time before they committed his body to the ground. Surprisingly, the calling hours were smaller than expected. Judging from the crowd, Tony was probably not the most popular kid in school, and his family was not a well-known family in the community. It didn't elicit much press, and it seemed as if the family was just as happy to not have an elaborate affair. They could have asked for anything, and Mr. DelGiorno would have given his best to arrange what they wanted; that was for sure.

As they pulled away from the cemetery that cold rainy day, Mr. DelGiorno couldn't shake the thought that although the light fanfare was touching and appropriate and the military service, Taps, the presentation of the flag, and twenty-one gun salute were all honors well-deserved, Tony's services had not nearly compared to any recent services for the latest Hollywood death. Superstars who, more often than not, killed themselves due to their own destructive personal choices. Yet those were the people who were idolized by the public and then given a far greater celebratory good-bye than Staff Sergeant Rusitani would ever have received. To Mr. DelGiorno, that was a damn American shame.

CHAPTER 20

S ure enough, Mrs. Updike, the person who had most recently appeared to Kathleen, was the next call for DelGiorno Funeral Home. She passed away in her sleep at Schuyler Hospital. Kathleen was beginning to get an uneasy feeling about her career choice. *How is it that I keep having these visions?* She kept deliberating the details in her mind. Mrs. Updike must have been at least eighty by now, so it was somewhat of a comfort that at least her visions were not about young children, so far. The people that she had seen were already old, most of them already sick, and probably all three had been ready to die. But why and how were they appearing to her? She wanted to confide in someone, but she just wasn't comfortable. It had actually been quite some time since her last vision, so perhaps it would never happen again. At least that was what she hoped.

Although Mrs. Updike had died at Schuyler Hospital, for some reason, they had requested a full autopsy, so that meant preparation would be long. An autopsy case was at least an hour longer than a regular embalming because all the internal organs were removed, therefore making it necessary to inject into a minimum of six different arteries rather than one, sometimes more, depending on how the flow of embalming fluid was. Hopefully the medical examiner left enough of the arteries exposed to find them easily. Some would cut them so short you had to dig to find them, making the process even more unbearable. Kathleen had let Johnny know about this inconvenience, so if he was assisting, he could at least help by leaving a little extra. Even though the embalming would take longer, the removal was at the coroner's office, which was a shorter trip, and Kath hoped she would run into Johnny while she was there.

When she arrived she didn't see Johnny, at least not where she was, and didn't want to ask for him to avoid him getting into trouble. She knew that everyone there had been overworked because of the investigations, so even if he was there, he probably should not be bothered. She figured they would catch up later anyway.

Once she returned to the funeral home and began to prep Mrs. Updike for services, in an attempt to keep her mind from the long process ahead, Kathleen reminisced about sixth grade in Mrs. Updike's classroom. She remembered being very afraid at first of having her for a teacher because she looked mean and pretty old, but as it turned out, she was a very caring woman. She had a beehive-type hairstyle, always up, and very long, pointy fingernails. Her current hair was thin and stringy; no way that her updo was going to be feasible now.

That year in sixth grade, Mrs. Updike had read the story *Caddie Woodlawn* aloud to the class, and Kathleen had loved just listening to the story. Mrs. Updike had also chosen a poem Kathleen had written to be read on the announcements, and she would never forget how proud she was of herself. It was a great esteem booster for a sixth grader and led Kathleen to write many more poems over the years. Her mother had written the poem on special paper in calligraphy then framed it, and Kathleen presented it to Mrs. Updike as a gift. She hadn't seen her in years and wondered if Mrs. Updike even would have remembered her as a student.

It took Kathleen nearly three hours to get the injection done, treat the viscera, and finally replace the skull cap and chest plate then stitch up the head and the large Y incision from shoulder to shoulder then down to the belly button. She was glad she didn't have to try to place the bag of organs back in the chest cavity. It usually never fit right again and made people look bloated in the chest and abdomen. Her father preferred to treat them with embalming powder then put it at the foot of the casket. That was where teeth went too when they didn't fit.

She laughed to herself when she remembered a recent event about a set of teeth that had fit but shouldn't have. Just as the family had arrived for the service of Mr. Jones, Kathleen received a frantic call from his place of death, explaining that they had accidently given the wrong set of teeth. Those teeth had belonged to another patient, who was still alive, and they wanted them back. No chance, Kathleen ensured her, as they were safe and snug in a corpse's mouth. Kathleen had contemplated calling the nurse supervisor at the facility because the nurse didn't seem to care where they had been, she just wanted them back, but still Kathleen refused. She never called the supervisor though, probably because she too had made mistakes and figured the nurse was already in enough trouble for losing the teeth in the first place.

When finished with the lengthy embalming, Kath decided to review the folder to confirm her suspicion about Mrs. Updike's age. She flicked off the prep room light and retreated to the office, where the files were kept.

Sure enough, Mrs. Updike was now eighty years old. Good prediction, but then again, Kathleen was pretty sharp with premonitions these days, wasn't she. At least if funeral directing didn't work out for her, perhaps she could read tarot cards or palms for a living.

She noticed that Mrs. Updike didn't belong to a specific church, and all the services were to be held at the cemetery only. A very old, very rural cemetery far outside of town. They made very few burials there anymore, and even the caretaker was about eighty. He still dug as many graves as he could by hand. Tomorrow would be the services with burial immediately after. She was surprised that Mrs. Updike didn't have any children, and it appeared that a friend had made all the arrangements. She wondered who approved the autopsy.

The doorbell startled Kathleen out of her trance. *Who could that be?* They weren't expecting anyone, she was pretty sure. Her dad wasn't there, so she hoped whomever it was needed something she was comfortable handling. As she pulled back the heavy oak door, there stood a feeble old man with a cane and fedora hat. He couldn't have been much taller than five feet tall, indicating a strong wind could surely have blown him over, cane and all. He didn't appear to be distressed or grieving as he beamed an enormous smile to greet her. "Hello," she responded as she opened the screen. "What can I do for you today?"

"I'd like to speak to the funeral director in charge," he replied gleefully.

"Okay then, that would be me at the moment. I am Kathleen DelGiorno," she explained as she reached out her hand to introduce herself. "My father and I are co-owners of the firm."

That sounded pretty important, Kathleen decided, and it was the first time she had actually spoken the words to someone.

"Well, this isn't what I was expecting, but if you are a funeral director, then you're the one I need to see. I would like to plan my services, young lady. Getting up in years, you know, and need to be sure I take care of this for my family."

"Please come in and we can take care of most of the paperwork today. Are you planning to prepay? If so, that is something I must wait for my father to complete, but we can still fill out the entire obituary and service information together. He should be back by the time we are done."

"Fine then," he said as he staggered feebly through the door.

Kathleen offered to take his hat, but he preferred to hold it, and as they sat at the desk, he laid it neatly on his lap. She began with the usual information—name, date and place of birth, education, and other vital statistic information that needed to be recorded on the death certificate. Her father had files that made the work easy as it mimicked the exact form of the death certificate itself. She then moved to the obituary information, gathering details about his life and family that would be included in the newspaper. As she inquired about a church, he paused for a moment then leaned in close, as if he wanted no one else to hear, even though they were alone. "I've got something to tell you," he nearly whispered, "but I am pretty sure it will surprise you."

"Okay, what is it?" She was a little concerned that it might be something she didn't want to hear based on his secretiveness.

"I am an atheist, young lady."

"Well, that is fine. Would you want someone to speak at your service? A friend, family member, or someone else?"

He looked a little disappointed with Kathleen's reaction. Perhaps he expected more, but really, it did not matter much to her. As a funeral director, she was used to wearing many hats. Although most of the funerals at DelGiornos were generally Catholic or Protestant, they basically conformed to the faith of the deceased, at least while dealing with the family. She remembered as a teenager finding her dad in a yarmulke for a Jewish service he was having. She remembered laughing at him, thinking it was silly that he had on this hat, until he explained it was an expectation of the job as a funeral director to respect the wishes and beliefs of those you served.

As she thought deeper about what Mr. Carter had said, she wondered why the word *atheist* sounded so cold and wrong as compared to the word Christian. That just rolled off people's lips as if they were paying someone a compliment. The word *atheist* sounded to her as if you were speaking of trash. Mr. Carter certainly was a pleasant man and had probably lived a moral life.

"People often ask me if I am afraid of going to . . ." His voice trailed off as he decided to point downward rather than say the word in front of a lady. "I always tell them no, because when you don't believe in God, you don't believe in heaven, and if there is no heaven, then no underworld either."

Interesting, she thought, and sensible too. She wondered if someone could be held accountable to burn in hell if they had never believed in either. Really, it wouldn't be fair. She thought about what the nuns who taught Sunday school in her youth would say about this or how they would react to this man. He was gentle and kind, worked hard, and seemingly led a good life that followed the Ten Commandments in his own way. He certainly was probably not a killer or thief, not likely to have coveted his neighbor's wife, and he seemed, so far as she could tell, to treat others fairly. How would a power like God judge him on his final day, or would He even be allowed?

She tried to pull her thoughts away from the topic, because since she had gotten back from college, she was already beginning to rethink some of her religious convictions. She didn't want to contemplate her beliefs even more just because a nice atheist had visited the funeral home today. She had enough problems with her premonitions as it was, and the comfort of her faith helped keep her from going over the edge for the time being.

As she tried to shake herself of these ideas, her mind then reverted to a recent pet peeve that had developed about religion. She hated the funeral services where the minister used the death as a tool to guilt people into being "saved." The typical "you can only get into heaven to see your loved one if you give your soul to Jesus right now." Of course they would go into the prayer of salvation, requesting that everyone close their eyes and repeat the words. It seemed like duress to Kathleen and certainly would be considered so in a court of law. "Raise your hand if you want the salvation and repeat after me," the minister would instruct. She always thought they wanted a raised hand so they could corner people in the back lot to get them to come to church.

Church had its place. She had seen firsthand that for some, their faith was the only resource for them to make it through the day, but she had relied less and less on her faith and had been okay, she thought. Was it because there was no God, or simply because He was taking good care of her during her time of doubt? Maybe she would never know, and really it would be too late when the time came for her own death.

She returned herself to the arrangements at hand and hoped Mr. Carter hadn't noticed her daydreaming while he carried on about his beliefs.

"Let's talk more about the services you would like, will you be buried or cremated?"

"I have a nice plot next to my wife. She died last year, and I haven't been the same since. I miss her dearly," he began as tears formed in his eyes.

She felt a little sorry that she had even asked, since it clearly elicited a bad memory for him. In an attempt to clear his mind, Kathleen continued to discuss all the service details. Just as they were planning to move to the showroom to look at merchandise, a casket and outer burial container for the cemetery, Mr. DelGiorno appeared. "Mr. Carter, hello," he greeted.

Kathleen was impressed that her dad had immediately recognized and recalled his name. That was common though, she knew. She had often heard her dad retell numerous stories about the funeral home, always referring to his clients by name no matter if he had buried them yesterday or decades ago. There was just something about the names becoming engrained, perhaps as part of their eternal memory.

"How have you been since Lillian's passing? What brings you in today?"

"Well, I've decided it was time I take care of my own arrangements, you know, so my children do not have to be burdened. Your daughter has done a lovely job for me, but I was wondering if I could have a word in private with you when we are done."

He gave her dad a wink, which Kathleen couldn't begin to imagine what it had meant.

"Sure thing. Kathleen, give me a shout when you are about done. You won't be able to sign the contract anyway, so I will finish from there. I'll see you shortly," he addressed both of them then left them to complete their work.

Once they finished up, Kath turned over Mr. Carter to her father for the final signatures and whatever else Mr. Carter wanted to discuss with her dad. She was ever so curious about what they had to chat about but didn't stick around to find out either. She was pretty sure she had done a fine job with Mr. Carter, so it couldn't possibly be a complaint about her. Obviously they knew each other, so it was probably nothing much. Kathleen was actually glad they had to catch up, because she was more interested in finding out if Johnny wanted to grab a bite to eat later.

Johnny and Kath decided to meet up for just a coffee that evening instead because he had to work late and didn't want Kath to wait to eat. It had been a couple days since they had seen each other because both had been busy with work. Now that Johnny was the full-time ME's assistant, he had more unpredictable hours. Kathleen certainly had no room to complain as she knew her schedule too was often erratic. It was good that they would have that commonality to balance their relationship. They would both have to get used to the other having to change plans unexpectedly. At least this way, neither could feel slighted as it would be happening both ways.

Kathleen was surprised when she finally laid eyes on Johnny. She could tell he was not himself. His eyes clearly had seen little sleep lately, and he looked as if he had been run over by a truck. She immediately embraced him and gave him a long kiss. This did seem to bring about a bit of sparkle in him, for which she was glad. "So relieved to get my hands on you," he whispered in her ear then grabbed her closer and took a long breath of her hair. "I have so needed to see you."

"Tell me about it. I have been thinking about you nonstop. By the looks of you though, it is sleep you need more than me." She smirked jokingly, trying not to hurt his feelings even though she was dead serious.

"We had to start some surveillance at Clear Rivers and Schuyler Hospital. Since our first case, we have gotten an unexpected lab back and discovered another poisoning. The only problem is that the patients are from two different facilities, which do not have any connections to the same doctors and nurses.

"It's fucking crazy," he continued, barely taking a breath. "Now it seems that it is a random killer rather than a serial nurse or doctor.

It is going to take a while, but at least we have a lead with the poison type. It appears that this person is injecting methanol directly into people's veins. It is a fast-diluting solution, so if the autopsies are not done rather quickly, often there is not trace. Not to mention, that both of the victims were elderly and terminal, so our only break is that the families of these people actually requested the autopsy. There could be more, many more, in fact. Right now, we are just trying to put together any connections between the two victims, but no luck so far."

She could tell that the events were weighing heavily on his mind. His compassion made him even more attractive to her. He reminded her so much of her dad, his commitment to help others and concern for the people he served, even though they were dead. She admired these traits in her dad and him as well. She remembered learning in a psych class that women will often end up with men that have similar personalities as their fathers, and she could surely see herself married to Johnny someday.

"Jesus, Johnny, it sounds awful. Is there anything I can do?"

"Indeed there is," he spoke gently as he leaned in to kiss her once again. "How about you just come home with me and chill. I could really use a quiet night with a beautiful girl. I am not on call tonight, so all I want to do is hold you and catch up on my sleep."

There was no way she was going to turn this offer down. She needed to chill too. She wondered for a minute if tonight might be a good time to confide in Johnny about her own problem—her visions in the rearview mirror. She was honored that he trusted her enough to discuss his problems with her and was certain he'd understand her problem too. Maybe she'd just have to see how the night went. After all, he needed her right now more than she needed to confide. He obviously was worse off at the moment.

She thought about the next day's work. They had afternoon services for Mrs. Updike. Dad wouldn't need to be up early and liked to sleep in when he could. She would take a gamble and spend the night with Johnny then sneak back home early before anyone else was up, and if by chance her dad did call in the middle of the night for a removal, she could always just claim they were up late, talking. It made things a little more exciting just thinking about getting caught.

CHAPTER 21

Kathleen's plan worked, and she made it home before anyone was out of bed. She guessed that her parents must have gone to bed early and probably never even noticed her missing. As she turned through the kitchen to go to her room, her cover was blown. She landed face-to-face with her mother, and surely Mom would recognize that Kathleen was still wearing the same clothes as she had on last night when she left.

Just as she was searching for the right words to say, she was saved by the bell. It was the funeral home line. She could tell because it had a slightly different ring than the home phone. "I'll grab that!" she shouted in apparent relief of not having to give an explanation, at least for now.

A new call, and although she did not get much sleep last night, it would buy her some time before she would have to face her mom or dad and provide a story about her arrival home at 7:00 a.m. She'd take off right now for the removal and be long gone before her dad got up. Surely she could come up with something, a long night with a girlfriend due to a breakup, or a late-night party where she had stayed to be the DD. So many excuses began to run through her mind she had to force herself back to the conversation happening on the phone. "Okay, I will contact the hospital and take care of bringing your mother back to the funeral home immediately. Have you and your family made any decisions about the type of services you would like? We will need permission to do the embalming if you are planning any public services."

"Yes, we would like mother to have a viewing. We would like to meet with you today at one o'clock. It is the only time that my brother and I can both be there."

"One will be fine. When you come in, plan to bring her clothing. We recommend undergarments, tops with long sleeves, and no low necklines. Shoes are optional, but feel free to bring them if you prefer. We will put all clothing you bring on your mother."

"Shoes won't be necessary. Mom has no legs."

She hoped he was kidding, but based on the odd silence on the phone, she knew he wasn't. *Open mouth, insert foot,* she thought—*no pun intended.* She could tell her lack of sleep was not going to be on her side today. It had been a while since she had made a stupid mistake at the funeral home, but it appeared she was once again on a roll. As she completed her conversation and hung up the phone, she realized she was in even deeper than she first imagined. She had overscheduled because not only had she just confirmed one o'clock arrangements, but Mrs. Updike's burial was scheduled for that exact time. *Oh shit!* She realized she had also forgotten to get a phone number for the family contact. Her only saving grace may be that her dad would be mad enough about these mistakes that he would not remember to give his disapproval about her not coming home last night.

At least the removal and embalming went smoothly. It went much quicker being that Mrs. Lewis was two limbs short of a full cadaver. She also still had to dress and do cosmetics and hair for Mrs. Updike. They always waited at least a day following an autopsy embalming to make sure as much tissue as possible had time to dry out, just to be on the safe side. Leakage would spread over clothes so quickly, and even the smallest amount could make it look like bucket loads and cause an enormous stain.

She did all that she could with Mrs. Updike's hair and even though it would be a closed casket, she felt it would be right to paint her nails. Mrs. Updike always had her hair and nails done. It was the last thing she could do for her. As she leaned over her hands, all she could think about was a hand coming up to grab her, holding her in a firm grasp until Kathleen would explain how she had brought her to her death through her vision. She decided one coat of polish would be enough this time, and rightly so.

By the time Kathleen emerged from the prep room she had very little time to get a shower and still be available to load the hearse for Mrs. Updike's funeral. She still hadn't seen her dad yet to let him know that he had arrangements at the same time as the burial.

As she shifted from the funeral home over to the house, she was practically on a run. She really was wishing that she had had more sleep last night but accepted the fact that she had only herself to blame. Her lack of sleep surely contributed to her runaway imagination. Fearing a corpse would grab her was ridiculous, and she knew that.

As she passed through the kitchen again, she made eye contact with her dad and waited for a comment regarding her inability to find her way home last evening. Nothing. Odd, she thought, but perhaps her mom had decided against telling him. That would surely be a break she needed, especially today. She would talk to her mom later and explain, but knowing that her dad was not aware would for sure make the day go smoother. "Dad, the family of our new call, Mrs. Lewis, could only come today at one o'clock so that both of her children could be here. I didn't want to disappoint them," she lied, "so I went ahead and scheduled. I figured at Fairview, I would be able to get close enough to the grave to manage the casket with just me and the vault guy."

She was a little astonished about how her lie was coming together so easily on the fly. Surely if he were to inquire about her late night now, a great excuse would come out with ease. Before he could show his dissatisfaction, she turned quickly and headed straight for the shower. "I'll be right down to help casket Mrs. Updike. I have already finished Mrs. Lewis' embalming. I love you, Daddy," she added to help ensure he could not possibly become angry with her.

Hot shower, hardly any flowers to pack up, and a graveside-only service, her day was beginning to look up. As she drove to the cemetery, she actually decided to listen to the radio but made sure it was an appropriate channel. Something of a respect thing, no hard rock or rap with a client in the car.

Soon the radio belted the upbeat tune of "*I can see clearly now the rain has gone.*"

She began to sing along and tap on the steering wheel as she thought about getting together again with Johnny. The ride to the cemetery was long and consisted of mainly dirt roads due to its rural location. Kathleen had only been there once and was so engrossed in her song that she had missed the turn. She gradually slowed the hearse down to pull into a driveway as she continued to sing along to the tune.

She needed a drive wide enough to make an easy turn with the hearse. Ensuring no ditches on either side to remove any doubt of error in backing up the beast. As she found a suitable driveway, she hoped no one was home, looking out in panic, thinking the grim reaper had arrived for them.

With a casket in the back, the view out the rear was even more hindered. As she pulled the shifting lever back to reverse, she checked both ways for cars, nothing. She slowly lifted off the brake and glanced up to the rearview to watch her descent out the drive. As her eyes fixated, her mind was telling her to look away, but she was almost frozen, glaring into the mirror. At once, there was a flash of light then a vision, this time a man, someone she did not recognize; however, his features would not soon be forgotten. His deep-set eyes almost twinkled, and he flashed a caring smile that made the whole experience creepy. She moved her eyes to her side mirrors and backed quickly out of the driveway, then peeled toward the cemetery just to be with someone alive. She nearly took out a headstone as she careened toward the vault truck. *Get me the hell out of this car.* As she darted out of the hearse, she almost tripped over herself getting to the man in waiting.

"Hello, Ms. DelGiorno." Ron, the vault guy, extended his hand to address her but was also ready to catch her just in case.

"Hey, Ron, listen we got busy this afternoon, so Dad couldn't make it. Do you mind backing the hearse up to the grave for me? We're going to need it closer to unload. You know how bad women drivers can be." She smiled flirtatiously to ensure she'd get her way.

There was no way she was getting back in that car to use the rearview. The car would be headed in the right direction when they were done to just pull out. She could hardly wait to get out of there already.

Just as they secured Mrs. Updike on the cemetery lift and placed the flowers around the grave, a few cars pulled into the cemetery for the services. An older man scampered up to the grave site. As he approached, Kathleen was just beginning to relax a little and realized that it was a beautiful day to be outside enjoying the last few nice days before fall.

He introduced himself and explained that he had been appointed to deliver the graveside service for Mrs. Updike. He had been a neighbor and friend for many years, he revealed. Kathleen looked for signs of his religion, a Bible, cross necklace, but could find nothing obvious. When she confirmed all guests were present, she gave him a nod to begin and stepped away from the grave a little, strategically into a spot where there was sun shining through the very old oak trees that lined the graveyard.

He thoughtfully moved closer to the grave then propped himself upon a large tombstone near the head of Mrs. Updike's plot. He was short enough that sitting there he almost reminded Kathleen of a hobbit on a toadstool. She felt guilty for thinking such a thing. He began his service discussing eternal life, and Kathleen was beginning to believe that this would indeed be a religious service, but his words quickly changed her mind.

He went on to discuss how everyone left treasures and jewels throughout their time here on earth. He described that with every person we met, each person we loved, we left something for them to remember us by. Perhaps it was something one taught to them, a recipe shared, a laugh, a story, or simply a friendly smile on an otherwise awful day. For some, treasures left were large; for others, very small. The jewels left behind, he explained, could be rare or perhaps very common, but indeed, they were left in many places, and each was a piece of the treasure chest that would lead to a person's eternal life here on earth.

He went on to confirm that if indeed someone touched a life, they would continue to live on in that person they touched in some way or another. Maybe a joke that person continued to share, a piece of knowledge they learned and passed on, a mannerism they inherited from the deceased, a moral they instilled to others, the love that they shared. In this way, people would remain here eternally with those who were left behind even though they were gone. As each of these jewels were distributed, a person would have instilled their treasures for people to share with more people, therefore living on through all the people they touched—eternally here until those treasures faded away, got lost, or stolen. Eternal life was what all should be striving for and could have, he concluded, as long as people continued sharing their jewels.

Kathleen wasn't sure if the sunny day or the beautiful sermon made her feel better, but she surely agreed that Mrs. Updike had accomplished eternal life with her good deeds and treasures she left behind. Hadn't Kath indeed keep her memory alive just yesterday as she recollected the treasures she had shared with her during her time in the sixth grade. In fact, Kath could imagine reading the *Caddie Woodlawn* story with her own children someday, passing on the treasure that Mrs. Updike had left with her. A ruby perhaps, Kath thought, as the cover of that book had been red.

As she pulled away, looking back in the rearview with no fear, she recalled as sense of peace that had overtaken her. She had never left a service feeling so confident in her beliefs or so comforted by the meaning this unknown man had just bestowed about eternal life. It wasn't a game or a farce, about the amount of money given to church, about what you believe or who you believed in. Eternal life was about the good you did on earth, and all could have it if they tried. She drove right straight from the cemetery to church to say a prayer and confess her sins.

CHAPTER 22

The first removal of the day was easy compared to the second. Even though it could have been a disaster, it turned out to be something they would have a good laugh over later on.

Kath and Mr. DelGiorno had arrived at a small, tidy Cape Cod home in a neighborhood just a few blocks away from the funeral home. The treelined neighborhood made it almost difficult to imagine that someone lay dead in a home somewhere along this docile strip. The middle-aged woman who answered the door had silvery hair and looked very distinguished. Once her dad made initial contact to let the family know the funeral personnel was there, he came back to the hearse to get Kath and the cot. It was protocol to not just arrive at a doorstep with a cot announcing your entrance. It would not only be rude to the family, but more importantly, it gave the director a peek inside as to what would be in store for them.

House removals were always a pain, and more times than not, it was up a set of stairs, in a narrow hallway, or worse, someone wedged between the tub and toilet after taking a nose dive off the john after a hard squat. No way could scientific gravity pull them in the opposite direction where they would just sprawl out to the floor, easy to remove. They had to lean toward the tub, a magnetic force of some sort perhaps that drew them in that direction. Of course, they always went face-first too, thereby allowing the blood to pool in their face, making them bloat and blue to look like Violet from Willy Wonka's Chocolate Factory. Never a good thing.

This time, her dad had come out confidently because he had caught a glimpse of the deceased right there inside the front door in a hospital bed. First floor, direct route, easy removal. As they moved into the living room, the middle-aged woman had slipped back into another room to retrieve something. The corpse looked peaceful. She was old and perhaps, based on her emaciated look, pretty sick as well.

As they cozied up the cot up to the bed and looked for the remote to raise the hospital bed to cot level for an easy move across, the silvery-haired lady returned.

"*No, no, noo!*" the woman shouted. "That is my mother, she's alive! Aunt Lucy is in the bedroom."

Disaster averted, no harm done. When Kathleen and her dad pulled off that block, they laughed until they both cried. The mother never even awoke the entire time they were there, and they were relieved to know that if and when she died, it would make for an easy removal. They had also hoped that now that Aunt Lucy was dead, they would still leave the mother in the front room for easy removal in the certain near future. Of course, their jokes were never meant to be disrespectful; they were simply a way of keeping things light in order to not dwell on the death that was so present in their existence.

They had just barely gotten Ms. Lucy back to the funeral home when the phone rang again. Another house removal. They moved quickly to get Lucy on the prep table so that they would not keep the other family waiting too long. Most families wanted the body removed from the home quickly after the death, but there was an occasional group that would want them there for hours to say good-byes and such. Kathleen never quite understood how people of the past were so comfortable having their loved ones laid out in their homes. She was glad things had evolved so that the funeral home became the hot spot for viewings.

Years ago, people were even laid out on couches in the home at times, the funeral director's role having been much different. They had portable equipment that would be hauled to the homes of the families; chairs, flower stands, candles, and sometimes even embalming machines. From pictures she had seen, the viewing was still set up similar to how it was now in the funeral home. Candles at each end of the body, flowers at the head, foot, and behind. It only made sense to her that bodies were now laid out at the funeral homes, at least there, a funeral director could keep tabs on the body, check for leakage, and reapply cosmetics under privacy. Just the thought of moving all that equipment every time they had a call was enough to make her tired.

Kathleen recognized the name of the new call but couldn't put a face with it. The deceased's name was Mr. O'Brien, and his wife had called to report the death. She had gone to school with several O'Brien kids, so perhaps that was why the name was familiar.

Once again, the call was near their neighborhood, just a few blocks away, but in the other direction. Perhaps they were living in Death Valley today, she thought. As they approached the house, there were no cars outside other than the coroner vehicle. Sometimes at house removals, there would be hordes of relatives, crying and carrying on. It was best when there were few people there in the unlikely event you ran into problems. More often than not, families were in the way and made the removal more awkward.

Once again, her dad approached the home first, and Kathleen waited for his signal to join him. This time, her dad directed her toward a side door that led right into the kitchen. Odd, Kathleen thought, but it was a ranch home, so perhaps the bedrooms were next to the kitchen.

They passed the coroner on his way out. An arrogant chap who barely spoke as he passed. "All set, get a hold of Dr. Parker to sign the certificate" was all he said. He scattered like lightning, knowing what was in store for them inside and knowing for sure he didn't want to assist in any way. As he went to his car, Kathleen noticed the small bag he was carrying, surely the blood draw kit that Johnny had mentioned

As they entered, there was a distinct smell of food that waved them through the door. It was delightful, and on the counters, there were so many cookies and muffins it was as if they were walking into a bakery.

Mrs. O'Brien was busily going about her work, nearly ignoring them as she pounded and chopped at what appeared to be squash. She obviously was in a hurry to prepare whatever it was she was making. *Was she expecting company?* Probably, Kathleen rationalized; most families usually would have company when a family member died.

As her dad led the cot around the kitchen island, there on the floor half sitting up was Mr. O'Brien. Apparently he had died right there in the kitchen, but it did not seem to bother his wife in any way. As Kathleen looked back at her then again at Mr. O'Brien, she quickly realized by his unique features that this was the man she had seen in her last vision. Stunned, she tried hard not to look surprised and give away her secret. She waited for her dad's lead, because she had never removed a body directly off the floor yet. At least she knew now they could lay the cot on the floor and get it back up thanks to Pete's lesson at the morgue months ago.

Mr. DelGiorno spoke quietly as he instructed Kathleen to lower the cot simultaneously with him. Then he turned to Mrs. O'Brien and asked her if she would like to leave the room. "No time for that, I will have family swarming the place soon, need to keep this food going."

Although odd, Kathleen could somewhat understand her desire to stay busy to keep her mind off the death, although this was a little extreme. Kathleen could tell that her dad purposefully turned his back toward Mrs. O'Brien to shield whatever he could the best he could. Touching, she decided. Mrs. O'Brien never looked up from her squash and pounded and chopped as if she were a contestant of *Top Chef* on a deadline.

The stature of Mr. O'Brien helped make this removal a little less traumatic. Although Kathleen had seen a much healthier vision of him, she could still tell it was him, and she could also determine he had been very sick lately.

After they had placed him on the cot her dad carefully strapped each buckle and pulled tightly then pulled the corduroy body bag over the top of Mr. O'Brien, zipped it up, then neatly folded the edges to make everything look presentable. Just as they had laid the cot down together, they lifted simultaneously to release the legs beneath it. Mr. DelGiorno wiggled the cot slightly to ensure it was locked upright, and they proceeded toward the door. "I appreciate your help, Mr. DelGiorno. You know he was very sick. He didn't want to live like this any longer. I couldn't blame him. I just wish the old coot would have been smart enough to keep his ass in bed. Dying right here in my kitchen, leaving me one last mess to clean up. I thought it would be over quicker, no time for him to get up out of bed."

Mr. DelGiorno tried to ease her mind, or perhaps change the subject. "Mary, he probably wanted to say one last good-bye."

"Either way, I got food to cook, and you got a body to get ready, so get on out of here." She demanded in a playful kind of way. "I do thank you though"—she stared right at Kathleen—"and he is out of his misery."

Her final comment seemed odd to Kathleen. *Why was she looking right at me, did she know about my visions? Was she thanking me for perhaps willing Mr. O'Brien to die?* No way had Kathleen done that—not on purpose, at least. She was so uneasy she wanted to blurt it to her dad but then thought better of it. After they loaded into the hearse, the radio once again played the tune—*"I can see clearly now the rain has gone."* The lyrics rushed through her head, but this time, they were changing almost through someone other than herself, and she silently sung along to the beat.

> I can see clearly now, your death is near,
> I saw your faaacce staring in my rearview mirror.
> Death will be present for you very sooooon.
> It's gonna be a dark, dark, dark, dark death-filled
> day.

She had always been good at making up new words to songs, but this was damn ridiculous. She switched off the radio and tried to make conversation to get her mind off the foolish lyrics she had just created without putting any thought into it. *Was this part of my telepathic gift?* She had already made up her mind that as soon as they had the both bodies embalmed, she would Google information on the paranormal. Johnny was on call tonight, so they probably weren't going to make any plans anyway.

If these crazy visions continued, she would need to see a doctor. Maybe there would be a story or something she could find that would explain all this. She felt as if she were on an emotional roller-coaster ride with too many hills and close calls. Between her visions and mini breakdowns, she was beginning to question her own sanity. She just wanted get to the bottom of these crazy forewarnings.

She had never really believed in ghosts but still hoped she would uncover something. After living in the funeral home for so many years, only once had she even remotely encountered anything ghostlike, at least not until her visions started.

The other instance occurred only because her friend Sally had brought a Ouija board to a sleepover she had for her eleventh-birthday party. They had supposedly contacted a boy who had been buried by her grandfather, and still to this day, Kathleen always figured Sally had been moving the planchette piece across the letters, but even so, that night she was creeped out by the whole experience.

They had asked the spirit they contacted if he was stuck in purgatory because of his terrible death, to which he replied yes. A drowning, he had told them, and his name was Jonathan Jonson. An odd spelling, but Sally had said that the Ouija would often have incorrect spellings. Sally claimed to be an expert on the game. The fact that the boy was eleven freaked the girls out even more. Kathleen was always going to go back and search the old funeral files for his name but never had. It wasn't going to happen now either. She had enough to worry about.

She remembered all the girls at the party had been so scared that after they played they never went to sleep. Kathleen made Sally take the box right out of her room and told her to never bring it back the house. Now she wondered if it were real, if perhaps she was some kind of a medium for the dead.

After finishing up her work for the day, she finally found some time to escape to her room. She sat at her computer and was amazed at the number of topics and pages filled with information on the paranormal. She was shocked by the number of hits she got just plugging in the words *premonitions about death.*

She did a search for articles on ESP; she looked at stories about people who could predict the future and others who claimed they saw or even talked to ghosts. She came across many interesting and disturbing stories and learned a lot about spirits and theories about premonitions, but nothing seemed to compare to or explain the visions she had been seeing. Most of the stories about people who had death premonitions were either of their own death or about people very close to them, like family members or best friends.

She was seeing something very different. Although she casually knew some of the people in her visions, she had never seen Mr. O'Brien before in her life. After hours of searching and reading, she gave up with no real hope or answers. She had come to the realization that she would have to find her own ways to deal with this burden. She also hoped that maybe something good would come of this. Maybe she could find a way to channel this gift to help others in a better way. Maybe there was a reason that would come to light to explain it all.

Her desire to quit searching was also cut short by her craving for something sweet. As she returned to the kitchen, the doorbell rang, and there stood Mrs. O'Brien, presenting her with a fresh squash pie. *Was this too a premonition?* She almost felt guilty taking the pie in the event she had somehow killed Mrs. O'Brien's husband, even unintentionally. However, her sweet tooth got the best of her. She thanked her graciously and immediately cut a huge slice and devoured it.

CHAPTER 23

The snow gently fell in giant flakes to the ground. Kathleen loved watching the lake freeze around the edges in the winter and also loved the look of the freshly fallen snow in the valley in which she lived. But even with the perk of beautiful snow, it also meant that cemeteries began to close, and burials had to be held over till spring. She never really felt it was fair for families to have to wait for the closure of death for sometimes months, but it was just the way it was. Families had to reopen the grieving process, which was harder for some than others.

The cemeteries claimed it took too much equipment and manpower to open a grave in the winter. Frost, they claimed, was too thick, although that defied what Kathleen had learned in earth science in ninth grade. A blanket of snow could act as an insulator so it would not push the frost farther into the ground. With heavy-duty equipment that was available today, they surely could enter the ground with the ease of a spoon through a Reese cup. Once they broke through the thin but tough top layer, they would be all set. However, it would also mean plowing all the driveways and ensuring no cars got stuck. Mr. DelGiorno believed the closing was more because the cemetery people did not want to be out in the cold, and perhaps he was right.

Regardless of the reasons, spring burials were also a burden to the funeral home because families always wanted to be there and often had to have yet another service, so to speak. The funeral homes often ran into scheduling problems because during spring burial season they not only had to deal with their present calls but also had to get families organized from past calls. Phone calls, grave openings, checks to vendors, vault orders, it was just a lot to add to the list, especially for busier firms. Kathleen dreaded the thought of her first season of spring burials, but that was still months away.

Instead, her mind went back to a happier notion, as she looked forward to the upcoming Christmas holiday, which was only two days away. She was excited to be home for Christmas with her mom and dad and even more thrilled that Johnny had been able to manage being off call on Christmas Eve and day. Now, if only they stayed slow at the funeral home, the holiday was sure to be perfect.

Not many other professions—doctors, nurses, coroners, and perhaps a few others were left with the commitment that often forced them into missing holiday events at the expense of their own family. Births and deaths took no holidays, that was for sure, and neither did the people who attended them as part of their job. There was always a bit of a black cloud that hung over the DelGiorno celebrations, and Kathleen recounted many a holiday where both she and her mother were hoping the phone would not ring and spoil the planned activities.

She decided that since it was snowing, it would be a great day to put on some old snuggly clothes and stay at the funeral home and do some cleaning. There were plenty of old boxes and bags of clothing left behind in the room just outside the prep room, and she had wanted to tackle it since she got home from college. She went to grab some tea then headed for her work.

The dust and sediment from years of just sitting idly on a shelf was overpowering at times. She coughed and choked as she moved things from the shelves to the garbage can she had dragged in from the garage. Every now and then, she would find a treasure, like a newspaper article highlighting her great-great-grandfather. He stood in the front of the funeral home when it was stilled called DelGiorno Cabinet Making and Embalming. In the picture, she could see the archaic sign behind him. He was a slightly morbid-looking character, not at all as gentle looking as her father.

During her adventure, she found a couple of old glass eyes and a few sets of dentures that she thought could be used for some awesome April Fools jokes. She loved April Fools Day and had often looked forward to playing a prank on her father. Her favorite, the year she filled the syrup bottle with T-gel dandruff shampoo and the shampoo bottle with syrup. Her dad nearly choked to death when he bit into the lovely pancakes she had thoughtfully prepared but laughed just the same at the well-executed trick she had played on him. She hadn't realized that he shouldn't have eaten the soap. She thought it was safe because she knew that some mean parents used to wash kids mouths out with soap. She had even been threatened with it once when she said school sucked.

She also found an old cat clock. She did not know for sure the era, it was probably sometime around the early seventies, she had guessed. Her dad would have been young then. Maybe it was his. It was a black cat, with the face of the clock on its belly. She looked for a place to plug it in to see if it still worked. As it started, the tail bobbed back and forth to count the seconds as did the eyes and ears in perfect time. Creepy, sort of, but still a good find. Perhaps she could get some money on eBay for it. Other than the clock mostly she found junk, stuff that should have been disposed of years ago.

She was nearing the end of her cleaning, and the garbage was just about full. She would probably need a forklift just to bring the garbage can back up from the basement. At least it had wheels, and there was a ramp. As she reached toward the last box filled with old garbage bags, her hand could feel the thick layer of dust that had collected. She grabbed hold of the first bag, noticing the contents were something hard and odd shaped. Maybe someone had wrapped old knickknacks of some sort to store down here. She untwisted part of the bag, and the newspaper wrap at the next layer seemed to confirm her prediction. She was pretty good at predicting things, but as she continued to feel around it, she really wasn't sure what it was. She reached in the bag to pull a package out. Perhaps she'd find another antique treasure.

Her mind quickly changed as she turned it over and read the tag attached to the paper, "This body part belongs to . . ." It looked almost like the name tags you got in preschool to identify your personal belongings. *What the fuck!* She felt around the paper a little more, and it became clear she was holding a foot. She looked back at the box and hoped that the remaining bags in the heaped-up box were still trinkets or something besides body parts. She reached for another and found the same. She dropped what she was doing, including the most recent body part pulled from the wreckage, and went immediately to find her dad.

After talking with her dad, she was a little bit relieved to find out that it was actually a normal occurrence. Because of religious beliefs, long ago, it was not uncommon for body parts to come to the funeral home to be surface embalmed and eventually buried with that person so they could return to the afterlife "whole." Obviously at times, for whatever reason, parts and people did not end up being reunited at death. Maybe they had moved, or maybe the family was unaware their part was still lingering behind. The possibilities were endless, but in any case, Kathleen was glad to learn that there was not a more psychopathic explanation for these random body parts being stored in the basement.

They had been there for years, long before even Mr. DelGiorno had graduated, and surely most everyone in the box had since passed. Either way, Kathleen, for her own piece of mind, would inventory the names just in case there was some way she could reunite a part with a long-lost soul. Even if they had been buried already, maybe the family would want to place the part in the grave or make a mold of the stump to use as a planter at the cemetery. She at least had to try to ease her mind.

She remembered a classmate at Simmons who had told a story about embalming a pair of legs for a diabetic lady, but those went directly to the cemetery lot to await her future demise. Thankfully this was another funeral tradition that had evolved to become more practical and even more ethical, perhaps.

The idea was not unreasonable because for some religions, it was unacceptable to be buried without all your parts in preparation of the resurrection. No one could go to eternity without being fully intact. She had heard stories about parts of sidewalks and roads being dug up if the blood of a Jewish person had been spilled on it just so it could be buried with them.

Her dad agreed that she could make an attempt to contact the families in the future, but only after he spoke to his attorney. There was nothing they had done wrong personally, but with today's litigation, even though nothing truly illegal had occurred, he certainly did not want to open a Pandora's Box. After Christmas, she decided, would be a good time for her to attempt to reunite families with their long-lost relative parts, and it would provide her a way for her to feel good about helping others as the new year began.

As she glanced at the kitchen clock, she could hardly believe that it was already dinnertime. It reminded her of the clock she had found in the basement, and she confirmed with her dad that it belonged to him in his youth. He got up to retrieve it from the basement and perhaps evoke some long-lost childhood memory.

Meanwhile, Kath decided that she had better get cleaned up and ready for Johnny's arrival. Her mom had invited him to dinner herself. Both her parents were very fond of him, and she could see why. She had had a couple of doozies for boyfriends in high school, including Chris Dunfee; he was just too wild, her dad insisted. They were glad she had settled for a hardworking, good-looking young man like Johnny.

CHAPTER 24

Sure enough, the next day, they had a new call. No chance it could have been yesterday or even a few days after the holiday. Something had to come up to ruin the holiday. And of course, it had to be the most demanding family of the year. They insisted on arrangements at their own home at 5:00 p.m. Just a couple hours before the DelGiornos would welcome the Pietrobini family for their first Christmas Eve dinner together. Kath decided to be the one to go because she had gone to school with one of the daughters. Maybe, once they realized they had a connection, it would take away some of the demanding edge they were already experiencing with the family, Kathleen hoped.

Unfortunately, that didn't help one bit. The family was loud, obnoxious, and rude. Almost as if to say, "Our Christmas was ruined, and so too will yours." The stubborn Italian in this family was very obvious. Kathleen was glad her own family was not quite as dominant. Must have been from a different region in Italy. Kathleen's mind could not help but wander from the dreary crampiness of their home to the carefully decorated rooms of her own spacious home. She wondered how they had ever gotten a moment's peace with such a large family having been raised in the tiny house.

As she sat at the Cantanos' house, she longed to be home with her own family. For sure, Mr. DelGiorno was getting ready to start the traditional fire in the fireplace in the front room of their house. They didn't often have a fire except near Christmastime. Jules was too afraid of it causing the house to burn down, even though back in the day, it was the main source of heat for the DelGiorno ancestors. To ease Jules's mind, Mr. DelGiorno had it inspected every year for safe measure. The Cantanos' home wasn't nearly as welcoming as her own. Her mother's taste and housekeeping was far superior to what she was exposed to at the moment.

Every time Kathleen thought they would be wrapping up arrangements, something new would come up. Usually a demand of sort. The wife and her children obviously did not like one another much, and the opinionated bunch had to hash out every last decision until all the others would concede. Kathleen tried to "direct" as much as she could, making suggestions, but trying hard not to come across as arrogant and spark more resentment from the family.

The last straw was when the family demanded they be allowed to smoke in the funeral home. They had been dragging and puffing on cigarettes all night long to the point of nausea for Kathleen. She couldn't take much more of them and had already spent nearly two and a half hours with them. Surely the Pietribinis were at her house by now, probably enjoying one of her mom's delicious rum eggnog delights with fresh cinnamon sprinkled on top and a peppermint candy cane to serve as a stir stick. She wanted to be there too! "Fine," she almost snapped, "I will close off a side room for only you and your family to smoke, but be aware that there is no ventilation, and it will be uncomfortable."

She knew they didn't really care about the ventilation as the haze in their kitchen was so thick it almost looked like the aftermath of an atomic bombing. Everyone was tired, and by now, even Kathleen was nearly as ornery as the rest of them. She didn't give a damn if her dad was mad; all she wanted was to be home with her family on Christmas Eve.

As Kathleen finally finished up arrangements, she followed the wife out to the living room where Mrs. Cantano turned to grab a family photo off the wall. As she took it down to hand it to Kathleen, a perfect square was left, outlined by years of nicotine embedded in the walls.

Kath took a deep sigh as she tried to neatly hang Mr. Cantano's clothes in the car. Then she sunk into the driver's seat of the bitter-cold Cadillac. Thank God for heated seats. Already she could smell the lingering cigarette smoke both on her clothes and the suit she brought to the car for Mr. Cantano. She turned over the engine and cranked up every heat mechanism available in the car. She hit the On-Star button and directed it to call home. Her mom answered. "On my way home, wait till I tell you about my evening. It was dreadful!"

"Okay, dear, our guests are waiting for you. Drive careful."

"Yeah, give them the heads-up that I will need to excuse myself for a quick shower. I just left a family of chain-smokers and smell like I've spent an evening in a brothel. I'll hurry though. I can't wait for an eggnog, extra rum," she teased.

She disconnected the call and pulled carefully out of the driveway but then sped along to get the hell out of there and as far away as she could from this family. It would be a couple of days before she would have to face them again, and because of that, she was finally able to become engrossed in thought about the events ahead this Christmas Eve.

As she approached the last traffic light before her block, she heard the screech of tires behind the Cadillac. Not tonight, she thought as she expected the lights moving toward her in the rearview mirror to soon be unseen due to the fact that they would now be in her trunk. She squinted her eyes in anticipation of the jolt, but instead of the whap she expected from behind, she simply saw the reflection of a person in the backseat. "Oh, Jesus," she spoke out loud. It was Mrs. Delabarto. She was the matriarch of one of the first families she had made arrangements with when she returned home from college. Her husband, Tom, had died and she and Kathleen had remained in contact often. Kathleen had visited her once or twice to drop off more thank-you cards and death certificates and always stopped to visit with her when she ran into her at the store.

This couldn't be. Kathleen knew she had just seen her a few weeks ago, a picture of health. Things were getting too weird, out of control, in fact.

Kath entered the house with a sense of uneasiness that quickly turned to pleasure the minute she laid eyes on Johnny. She would have to tell him about these visions. If she did not get these things off her mind or clear her head, she did not know where she would end up. When they had a few minutes alone, she would try to talk to Johnny. She tried to act calm and excused herself quickly for a shower. For sure, that would be enough to freshen herself up for the night ahead and hopefully inspire a better mood.

As she arrived in the front room refreshed from her shower, her mom handed her a made-to-order eggnog that she had been anticipating, complete with extra rum as requested. It seemed everyone was staring at her oddly. She glanced down to make sure she had dressed appropriately but found nothing unchecked. Just as she began to open her mouth about her most unpleasant evening, Johnny pulled her hand and led her to the fireplace, where the family stockings were glistening in the firelight. He dropped to one knee, and as their parents approvingly looked on, he asked Kathleen to be his wife.

She was dumbfounded, completely taken aback. Just a half hour ago she was living what she thought to be the most awful life, and here and now, all that was forgotten. Finally, the good that she knew existed wrapped around her so lovingly that she smirked for a brief minute, realizing the Cantanos couldn't ruin her entire evening after all, even though she was sure they had put forth their best effort.

Dinner was served, and the evening was a delight, with everyone catching up on lost time. Stories were shared about each of their parents' engagements and other special family events and traditions. Kathleen knew that the joining of their families would be like bringing together mashed potatoes with butter, cupcakes with icing, or bacon with eggs. It would be as if they belonged together always.

CHAPTER 25

More than two weeks had passed, but thankfully, no call had come in for Mrs. Delabarto. In fact, Kathleen kept checking the newspaper to see if she had gone to another firm, even though she knew that their family wouldn't choose another funeral home. She was actually feeling a bit of relief that one of her visions had been wrong. In fact, she needed to get a hold of Mrs. Delabarto soon and wish her a Happy New Year.

It was January the sixth, Kathleen's twenty-fourth birthday, but not such a happy one as they were preparing to bury the body of a young man who had chosen to take his own life just after Christmas. She would much rather be spending time with her family, but that was out of the question today because she was needed here for this family.

This was a call where a viewing was going to be out of the question due to the damage he had inflicted on himself. So close to Christmas, it surely was a terrible time for this sort of thing. This young man had driven his truck to the edge of a cliff, climbed out, and then shot himself. When Kathleen and her dad arrived for the removal, they were led by the coldhearted coroner to the edge of the hill to see a blood trail and body lying about twenty-five feet below.

As they surveyed the damage and calculated a plan to bring him back up, the coroner announced, "I got straps, but I am not getting them all bloody. When I was waiting for you, I noticed that he had some brand-new ones in his truck. His truck, his blood, we'll use his straps."

Kathleen had wished at that moment that Johnny had been on call so that someone with more compassion could assist them with the removal. She wasn't sure if her dad might push the coroner's ass right over the cliff, as she could tell by the look on his face that he was not happy with this comment.

Of all the different causes of death, her father was most affected by suicide, likely because his own closest cousin had hung himself when they were both in their early twenties, just starting out in life. His cousin had been depressed off and on for years, and Steve tried to keep in contact as much as possible. His cousin had even tried to reach Steve the night he died, but he had been out. He often wondered if he could have prevented it, at least that night. It had been a very difficult time for Steve, and he always was disturbed by calls that involved suicide.

Once the body was released, Kathleen had done all that she could to prepare the body so that her dad would not have to relive whatever horrible feelings that suicide evoked for him. She too was disturbed as she began to collect the personal belongings from his pockets, realizing that she was retracing his last hours by the receipts in his pocket. Stopped for gas, snack at McDonald's, then bought some ammo. She wouldn't normally ever tamper with belongings but felt she would spare the family some pain when she tossed that receipt into the medical waste.

There were going to be no public services at the funeral home. His mother had simply requested that she be allowed to come hold his hand, so a few days earlier, they arranged a private viewing, so to speak, and had brought Jonathan to a room by the chapel. He had been laid out on a portable prep table with a clean white sheet as a shroud to hide his disfigured head, but his hand lay outside for her to have one last moment with her son alone.

His mother had spent nearly two hours with him, and as she left the building, she could not thank the DelGiornos enough for their understanding and for allowing her this time.

It was the least they could do in their minds. At DelGiorno Funeral Home, they both made a point to ensure they did all they could to allow for a viewing, but in this case, it was beyond their repair. No amount of restoration would be suitable for this young man, but had there been any chance for it, Mr. DelGiorno surely would have tried.

As the boy's mother left the building on the day she came to say good-bye to her only son, Kathleen and her father both became teary-eyed as they turned over what little personal effects that were collected. It was only the second time ever that Kathleen had witnessed her father become emotional, and already she had seen enough. Her dad quickly left the room, and she knew better than to pursue him.

Later that evening, the only thing Kathleen could think about was how very lucky she was to have Johnny. She went to his house that night and made sure they were intimate so that he would never doubt how much she cared if something ever happened to her. She could not get close enough to him all night long and barely slept as she realized how very fragile life was indeed.

The burial service had been scheduled in early afternoon, so Kathleen held hope that the rest of the day would not be so gloomy. At the cemetery, the crowds came and went quickly, and before she knew it, they were in the hearse on the way back to the funeral home. They had been greeted at the garage by her mother. Not usual. She went on to tell them that the Delabarto family had just come by. Jenny Delabarto was ill, and her children were in the office, waiting to complete prearrangements.

Kathleen wanted to take care of this family even though it was her birthday, and she would much rather be drowning in cake about now. She quickly changed hats from suicide service director to prearrangement specialist and set about to greet the family.

As she entered the office, hugs were abounding. Although she had only met the Delabarto family when their father had died, they were grateful to see Kathleen again, comforted that she would be able to assist with their mom's arrangements too. They knew that their mother and Kathleen had kept in contact.

She quickly gathered what she would need to complete a file with them and sat to record her story. It turns out that Mrs. Delabarto had recently taken a turn for the worse, very unexpectedly. She was at Schuyler Hospital, and the doctors gave her only days. Kathleen was taken aback as she once again recalled seeing her just a few weeks prior. She offered her condolences and went straight to work.

The family was relaxed and in fact joked often about great memories they had of their mother. Kath was relieved that this was going so smoothly, given her last set of funeral arrangements, which included practically the same number of children, was a nightmare. She was working hard to forget her time with the Cantano family, and she knew this family was going to be much easier to handle.

As they continued with prearrangements and were near wrapping up, the family was pleased with their selections, and somehow having their dad pass more recently helped them to better focus on what their mom would want. Many of the service and merchandise selections were duplicated, with some minor changes to fit her unique personality.

The ring of a cell phone during the arrangements was not uncommon. Mrs. Delabarto's children had been talking back and forth with a few siblings who chose to stay behind at the hospital in order to keep their mom comfortable. The last time, it was the phone of her son Nick. He answered and paused briefly, as if he were searching for the right words, then announced to the entire room that mom had passed. Although expected, the reality that they were in the midst of making her prearrangements just a few minutes prior and joking about memories dear and near sent them all, including Kathleen, from put together to crying messes. This was the first time Kathleen had ever cried while making arrangements for a family, but it wouldn't be the last for sure. The family was very understanding as Kath explained that it was also her birthday and that she was honored that she would be spending her day taking care of their mother. She meant it too, and it also brought some comfort to them as well.

By the time Kathleen was done, she was completely burned out but was looking forward to a dinner out with Johnny for her birthday. It would be a well-deserved end to an otherwise terrible birthday. She struggled a bit with the idea that although she handled two families today who were dealing with the end of a life, she was moving on with the day to celebrate her own birthday.

Johnny arrived on time, and Kathy was eager to get into his arms even just for a brief second before they had to leave. They were planning to go all out at an upscale restaurant in the next town over. They rarely ate there because of the price and the fact that it was really out of their league in terms of status, but because they were to celebrate her birthday and their engagement, they decided to splurge. Kathleen's dad entered the front room just as they were about to leave.

"Johnny, you need a suit coat if you are going to Esperanza. They won't even let you in the door, son."

Kathleen knew that driving all the way back to his house would take too long, but she had an idea. As she cleaned out the basement a few weeks ago, she had come across several suit jackets that people would often donate for indigent funerals, and they were all in good shape. She ran downstairs, keeping in mind the color of his pants, shirt, and tie to be sure it would complement his outfit. She grabbed two just in case and went back to the front room to show her dad and Johnny. The first choice was perfect, fit as though it had been tailored just for him. As Johnny admired the fit, Kathleen's dad queried whom it had belonged to. "Oh, it says here Mr. Glacier. Didn't he die a few months ago, Dad."

"Indeed he did, and that coat there was his wife's first choice. After I had him all dressed and ready to go, she changed her mind, brought in a new suit, and told me to keep that one."

The look on Johnny's face went from delight to disgust in an instant flat. He wriggled his ass out of that coat so fast you'd have thought it was full of fire ants. Kathleen's dad nearly pissed himself on the spot.

"Jesus, that is not right. Why did you grab something that a dead guy was wearing?"

"How was I to know?" she insisted, trying hard to keep her laughs contained.

Once he gained his composure, he too began to laugh. She loved that he had a sense of humor and couldn't stay mad long. This she thought would go in their first family memory album. For sure, any time from this day forward that she looked at a photo of the two of them on this night, the jacket story would be sure to rear its ugly—funny, rather—head.

"Try this one, we have to get going, or we'll be late. Dad, this has no name, does that mean it is okay?"

"I am sure it is," he said as Johnny slipped on yet another perfectly fitted jacket. "You might want to consider modeling for the funeral catalogs. You must be standard man size."

It was getting way too deep and having become the butt of all the jokes, Johnny was eager to leave. They said their good-byes and headed out.

They were taking the Cadillac tonight; Mr. DelGiorno insisted Johnny and Kathleen arrive in style. Johnny was preparing to get in the driver's side, and the minute he landed his ass in the cushy driver's seat, he began to prance around in it like a stripper.

"What on earth are you doing?"

"Well, I am just checking out the shocks. We might just have to break in another DelGiorno funeral car tonight. Remember our first date?"

He smiled at her, and she couldn't help but begin to think of a place that they could perhaps pull into on their way home tonight.

Although more relaxed than he had been other times, as they drove Johnny began to talk about the investigation at work. He had mentioned that they had a few leads, but each had so far turned to a dead end. He made sure that his pun was not taken literally.

150

He continued to have to work long hours because they were still reviewing all tapes from at least two facilities and checking all sign in and out logs. It took hours, but Johnny was grateful for the overtime that was helping to fund tonight's outing as well as Kathleen's engagement ring. "Hey, did you guys have a new call this morning at Schuyler Hospital?"

"No, why do you ask? We got one today, but that was this afternoon. The family sat with me making prearrangements when their mother passed away."

"Just curious, I saw your dad on surveillance today. He didn't have a cot though."

"He was probably picking up some personal effects from a previous call or something. The hospitals are notorious for misplacing people's things."

She really couldn't imagine for sure why he would have been there, because they had not had a call at Schuyler in weeks until today when Mrs. Delabarto passed. It would have made more sense for them to call the family by that point. Maybe he had a friend who was sick; she'd have to remember to ask.

The ride was long to Esperanza, but she did not mind. It had been a while since they had been able to talk in private much, with the whirlwind of the holidays and people all around and the fact that they had both been working so much.

She reminisced about the events of Jenny's prearrangements and couldn't get the image she saw of her in the Cadillac weeks prior out of her mind. Kath glanced cautiously to the backseat to ensure they had not picked up any unwanted passengers. *Nothing. Good.*

"Johnny, I have something I've wanted to talk to you about, but I am not sure how to go about it." She could tell that his face was worried. "No, no, it's not about us, it's me actually. Some strange things have been happening to me that I have been afraid to share with anyone."

"Kathleen, please let it out, you know you can trust me. Whatever it is, why don't we try to come up with a solution together? Once we are married, all our decisions and problems will become each other's."

She couldn't help but feel very comforted by his sincerity. She went on to tell him everything, the days, the faces she saw, the circumstances in which they had each appeared, and the disturbing fact that they had all died, up until Mrs. Delabarto, almost instantly. He was a little sarcastic about the idea that one of her visions had occurred just following fabulous sex they had in the hearse. A compliment, he thought.

He listened intently and was careful about his reaction. He knew that it was a bit far-fetched, but Kathleen had no reason to lie about it. He was hoping she was not hallucinating or having a nervous breakdown or something. "Do you think you should see a doctor?" he asked. "Maybe there is an explanation that he could derive that would make it stop or at least make you feel better."

She didn't want to tell anyone else. Now that she had confided in Johnny, she already felt better about it. At least a little. A doctor for sure would think she was a whack job, probably prescribe her some drug with even worse side effects. She was already disturbed every time she saw or read a drug ad when the listed side effects were worse than the initial problem to start with. It was ironic how people had become so dependent on such quackery. It wasn't worth it to her at least. She would deal in her own way. "Updike, you said that you had a vision of Marion Updike, right? She is one of our poison victims. We just got the labs back this week."

"I was wondering who ordered her autopsy. A woman who was eighty and in a hospital shouldn't have needed a full autopsy."

She was trying to reassure herself that Mrs. Updike must have been sick to ease her mind. Up until now, she believed that the visions she was having were truly just coincidences of pending deaths of very ill people. She did not even want to begin to think that she could somehow cause a perfectly healthy person to drop dead.

"Well, she was actually in for a routine procedure, nothing life threatening, then all of a sudden, she was dead. They had to order one."

He explained how the office had been very busy reviewing labs too. Once they had discovered the type of poison and determined it could be found in the bloodstream if it were soon enough after the death, the ME office arranged for several hospitals and nursing homes to collect blood samples. On a regular basis, the coroner had been contacting families for permission to just do a blood draw following the death of many patients. "It is going to help us nail the bastard a lot quicker now. Most families we have approached have been pretty cooperative."

"Great, so now I am faced with the fact that not only am I willing the people I see to die naturally, I'm actually willing the murderer to kill the people in my visions. That's a comfort."

Maybe I really do need some drugs, regardless of the side effects.

CHAPTER 26

Kathleen woke up early on Saturday morning, reeling in pain. Her abdomen was cramping, and she sighed at the idea of her monthly beginning today. She and Johnny had plans tonight, and she had been craving a little intimacy. As she pulled back the covers and whirled herself out of bed toward the bathroom, she could feel the warm flow begin to pool and run heavily downward, and she quickened her pace down the hall. Already she could feel the moisture that confirmed that it had seeped through her underpants and pajamas. *Damn it,* she thought. She had on her favorite pj's, and it was not likely the amount of wetness she felt would wash out. As she reached the bowl and began to disrobe, the amount of blood that she saw was disturbing.

The cramping continued to pulsate through lower abdomen and back. It was much more excruciating than any cramps she had experienced before, and the flow was so urgent that when she glanced into the previously clear bowl, it appeared as if someone had just finished an embalming on an elephant right there in the toilet.

Her mind raced between the jarring pain and a search for the date of her last period. She realized that it had been over two months. She contemplated the situation a little more and came to the understanding that this was more than her period; she must be having a miscarriage.

How could this be, why hadn't I realized I was pregnant? She had put on a few pounds but chalked that up to eating out with Johnny so much and to having her mother's great cooking so often. She recounted how busy she had been over the past few months with work, with Johnny, and with making some initial wedding plans with her mother. It made sense that she would not have noticed. Life was moving fast paced lately, and she surely didn't miss her menses. It just as easily could have been stress and overwork that had made her late. She and Johnny were always careful, and she could only recall a handful of times they took a chance. Obviously their gamble didn't pay off this time.

Kathleen went back and forth from grief to relief. It certainly was not at all a convenient time to be pregnant. She was just starting her career and learning the ropes of the funeral business. If she were pregnant, she definitely could not be in the embalming room and eventually wouldn't have been able to lift bodies either. On the other hand, this was their baby, a once-living being that she and Johnny had created even though not planned. She imagined what it would have looked like, the best features of each of them. She pictured Johnny's large round eyes with her dark-red wavy hair. She couldn't help but wonder if it had been a girl or a boy. Tears welled up in her eyes.

She counted the months in her head, and her grief again shifted back to relief. The baby would have been due around October, just months before their wedding. It would not have been convenient to have a two-month-old child to care for, and it would have certainly meant no honeymoon.

As Kathleen continued to feel light-headed, she hoped it was due to her overactive mind, not blood loss. She could not tell her mom or dad. What a disappointment it would be for them. They were strict Catholics, and this would not be well received in their circle. Even though she did not follow the same commitment to her religion, she still would not intentionally share this information with them. It was one of those "don't ask, don't tell" details that she'd choose to leave out of their conversations.

She reached across toward the sink to grab the hand towel. She needed to use it to stop the flow in order to walk across the room to the tub without turning the room into a scene from *Carrie*. As she stretched toward the sink, her straining extruded even more blood and created sharper cramps. She pressed down on her stomach and bit down on her tongue to avoid screaming out in pain.

Finally she felt the flow let up enough to move to the tub. She wanted to soak in a hot bath, but that was out of the question. A hot shower would have to do, and she stood in the tub as the water warmed so she would not expel on the bath mat. The steam of the shower was relaxing and helped her to calm down and take her mind off her situation temporarily.

She had forgotten to pull out a bath towel to dry off with, so she would be forced to grab the decorative towels from the rack next to the shower. Her mom would be pissed, but she would dry off carefully so not to stain it, then get a load of laundry started and replace it before she noticed.

Because her mom never worked outside the home, she was very meticulous about her housework and the tidiness of her home. She was a very particular designer and carefully planned each room in their house to make it welcoming and elicit compliments from all who entered. Kath was not nearly as creative when it came to decorating or planning, which was why she also enjoyed her mom's input for the wedding. She knew it would be perfect down to the last detail thanks to her mother.

Because of her haste to get to the bathroom this morning, she had no clothes to redress into. She would have to use the already soiled hand towel to prevent the flow from exiting as she went back to her room. She wrapped the larger bath towel around her and scurried to her room to get some clothes. She was definitely wearing sweats today, and she chose a dark pair of pants just in case she overflowed again. She put on her comfortable clothes, grabbed some Midol, and gathered up the clothes to be washed. She added them to another basket so it looked as if she were just doing a random load and set out to conquer the stains.

As she reached the laundry room unnoticed, she applied stain remover to her pj's in hopes that an Oxy miracle would get the stains out even though she knew it was very unlikely. She piled the rest of the basket into the wash and made a mental note of the time to make sure she returned to the load before her mother found it. She contemplated whether this laundry should be washed in the washer and dryer at the funeral home, where they washed the biohazard loads.

Her thoughts turned once again to the baby and the sadness she felt for the loss. She didn't think she should tell Johnny either, no need for both of them to be disappointed. Even though he probably was equally unready to become a parent just yet, he would still be sad, she knew for sure. He also had been under a lot of stress due to the investigation and needed nothing more to worry about. Especially something that no one could change now.

It was God's will, His way of letting her know that something must have been wrong with the fetus. That it probably would not survive had it made it to full term. She had seen enough sick children die over the years and took to heart her father's philosophy about the death of a child to help comfort herself. Other than accidents, which were always terrible, most of the children whom they had done services for over the years were sick and often better off once they passed for one reason or another. Down syndrome, cancer, and even one child with AIDS. The mother had made prearrangements for herself after her five-year-old son had died.

The most recent child death call, which was while Kathleen was away at school, happened because the mother was so high on oxy-cotin. The mom had left the burner of the gas stove on after she lit a cigarette and ended up asphyxiating her own child. The burner that was left on lit a plastic toaster that was sitting on the stove on fire. A toaster most likely put there by her child in order to make her own dinner of bread and butter. She was four. That stupid bitch mother lived, but thankfully, her child did not have to go through the trauma of living with such an unfit mother. No doubt that woman would likely be pregnant before long and put yet another child through the misery that she couldn't quite pull herself out of. Kathleen had a hard time accepting why God would let these things happen to innocent children, but there had to be a reason, and it was hard not to believe that many of these children would be better off with God up in heaven.

They had had many stillborn babies at the funeral home over the years. It was state law to require a death certificate and disposition of any fetus twenty-four weeks gestation or further along. It was always difficult for the parents, but most families would not have actual services, just a burial or cremation. The most recent stillborn they had had been the baby of a very young mother; in fact, so young her mother had to drive her to the funeral home. Clearly the young mother was not ready to take on the financial responsibilities of raising a child as she had still not paid the minimal two-hundred-dollar fee they had charged for the cemetery fees and probably never would.

Mr. DelGiorno never made a profit on an infant funeral. The rule was all merchandise charged at cost and no charge for use of the facility or livery, so the biggest expense was the third-party cash advances, such as the cemetery fees.

It was obvious this child would not have been brought up in a stable environment, and Kathleen actually had a bit of resentment toward this young girl for being so irresponsible for getting pregnant with no means to raise a child from infancy to college. If she didn't have two hundred dollars to bury her child, how the hell would she have bought formula, diapers, food, or even paid the hospital bill for the birth? Love was one thing, but really, without the means to provide the basics, people had no place to be having children. Chances were that her own inability to care for herself was perhaps the reason her baby did not survive.

Kathleen began to feel guilty again. Had she known she was pregnant, she would have been taking better care of herself. She had been very neglectful toward her health lately, that was for sure. Was she the cause of her baby's death? She felt like the Grim Reaper herself between the loss of this baby and the other visions she had been having, all of whom wound up dead. *No, Kathleen,* she reassured herself. *Something must have been wrong to begin with, natural selection, survival of the fittest. Keep believing that to ease your mind, because you are on your own with this one,* she told herself.

As a little girl, Kathleen had been curious and felt dreadfully sad whenever a child had died. She had always gone in the viewing room when no one was looking and talked with the children. No one ever knew she had done this, and she would never have told either because her mom and dad wanted to believe that they were sheltering her from such terror. At that time, she was too young to truly understand the reasons behind their deaths, but she had always wished she could have helped them. She felt terrible for their parents, and she had even imagined what her mom would do if she were no longer alive. Now Kathleen wondered how she had become so detached about a child's death; was it simply because so many of these children were suffering on earth? Perhaps that way of thinking helped her to deal with it.

Kath decided to find her father to let him know she was under the weather and would be in her room, resting, in case he needed her. As she passed through the hallway between their house and the funeral home, which also led to the garage, she, of course, laid her eyes on the black box. This was their baby removal case. A small black suitcase with silk lining inside. It looked very much like a medical bag that a doctor of the past might have carried to visit a patient at home. The stainless silver handles and locking hinges stood out on the black case like the chrome on a just-waxed vehicle.

Obviously, it would be ridiculous to remove a baby on a six foot funeral cot. It was a dignified way to remove a baby from the hospital without letting on to anyone who might pass by what possibly could be in the case. She actually would pretend she was a doctor when she carried it down the hall of a hospital, greeting people she made eye contact with to keep her cover. She was relieved by the reality that her miscarriage was by far a much easier way to lose a child. She could not bear the idea that it may have taken a breath or two then had to be placed in that black box.

She found her dad in the arrangement office, and he was apparently busy with paperwork. As she entered, he quickly closed up one of the folders he was working on and returned it to his bottom drawer, almost in a guilty fashion. She forgot about his odd behavior in an instant as her cramps began to present again. She wondered how long she would be suffering with this pain, hopefully not too long, but at least they did not have a service today. There was no way she would make it through a day of comforting others, not today.

"Hey, Sunshine." His demeanor indicated that he was hiding something although he was trying to act collected. "I didn't expect you to be in today."

"Actually, I am not coming to work. I just wanted to let you know that I am not feeling well. I'll be in my room if you need anything today. Must be the flu bug or something."

They both were being a little deceitful today, which gave her a bit of consolation as she flat-out lied to him. But she couldn't help but wonder what that red file he had so casually tried to return to the drawer had inside it.

"Well, get some sleep, it is pierogi day, and we have ordered three dozen to pick up later today. You won't want to miss them. I am sure your mom will pick up pork or chicken to serve with them."

He was absolutely right. Pierogi from the Greek church in town were a treat they enjoyed just a few times a year when the ladies of the church would get together to make thousands of the homemade traditional treats to help support the church. Stuffed with potato or sauerkraut and served with fried onions and drenched in way more butter than a person should be allowed to consume. She would only eat the potato, and her mom would fry them up so the outsides were just browned and crispy. Kath would make sure she made it to dinner even if she couldn't eat much.

The Greek Orthodox Church was a modest church built on a side hill with what seemed like one hundred steps to reach the top, and it was the only way in. They had been working on a building fund for years so they could move to a more elderly friendly location. It was difficult for even a young person to make the trek up the stairs just to attend services. The hill was so steep that a ramp would be impossible to engineer or install. Kathleen was sure they had considered all options that may have made it easier to get to, especially now that most of the congregation of the church was elderly.

Getting a casket up those stairs was nearly an impossible feat, and they always made it clear to families they needed exactly six strong men to carry. Any less would be too little manpower; any more would be tripping over each other. The casket would be nearly at a forty-five-degree angle going up the stairs, and one wrong move or trip would surely have resulted in disaster. No doubt the stress in the pallbearer's faces was always evident as they climbed toward the top, each likely saying their own prayer of hope that they would make it to the crest alive themselves. If it were winter and there was the least bit of snow on the stairs, everyone was on edge until the casket would safely arrive and get wheeled through the vestibule.

Although she hated that part of the services at the Greek Church, once inside, the beauty of the ceremony made up for it all. She had often imagined how pleasing it would be to attend services there more often. Just like the Catholics, much of the service rituals were the same for every funeral, but instead of being spoken, they were chanted by the cantors. Obviously the priests were well trained in singing rather than saying the sermon.

The low voice of the pastor echoed through her mind as she imagined she was there now. The singing voice emphasizing and drawing out each note.

Eee-terrr-nal memmm-or-ies, eee-terrr-nal memmm-or-ies. For-ev-er and ev-er . . . Am-en. She certainly did not know all the words, but some parts always stuck with her, and the ones she knew, she would sing under her breath, just as she would repeat the Hail Mary at her own church.

As she passed back through the kitchen, her mother was there, reading the newspaper. Kathleen needed her support, and while she couldn't tell her why, she reached out and gave her mom a big hug, knowing she would get one in return. She wanted to feel the closeness of mother and child, and once she was in her arms, she felt immediate comfort. Her mom didn't question her, but it was obvious she knew Kathleen was hurting for some reason, mother's instinct.

She held her closer and whispered, "I love you, dear."

CHAPTER 27

By the next day, Kathleen was feeling much better, and she had even been able to scarf down more pierogi than she expected the night before. Her body had been craving carbs and protein, and she ate like a bear preparing for hibernation, surprising everyone at the dinner table.

She had the same famished feeling when she hit the breakfast table, and ate once again like a champion. She decided that she would definitely attend the morning Mass. She needed her faith to help her through her little secret. God already knew, so she would have someone to talk to about it, and that made her feel better. When church was over, she would make a trip to the drug store and pick up some vitamins and condoms—two things she needed in order to better take care of herself. The day looked bright, so she would ride to church with her parents, then walk back home, making her stops on the way. She'd have to use the chain pharmacy today because the hometown pharmacist attended her church, and she didn't want to be given the stare down when purchasing her birth control.

"Are you going to Mass this morning?" she directed her question to both her dad and mom even though she already knew the answer.

There were very few times she could ever recall them missing a Sunday Mass. They attended every Sunday as a family no matter what. Even a death call would be put on hold, as long as it wasn't a house removal, to attend church. Lately, Kathleen had not been as dutiful in attending. Her parents had been understanding about her position but always encouraged her to go nonetheless. "I am planning to go with you today. What time will you be leaving?"

"In the car by nine forty-five to ensure we can get a seat closest to God." He winked.

She still wanted her comfort clothes today but did have a dressier pair of pull-on pants that would be suitable for church. She couldn't bear to have pressure around her now obvious bloated stomach right now. As usual, she chose a shirt that was not black and slipped on a comfortable pair of flats with no stockings.

Father Paul was presenting Mass. Kathleen always enjoyed Mass given by Father Paul better than some of the other priests. He was a little less traditional and seemed to embrace the fact that with society changing, so should the religious expectations of the church adjust to meet the lifestyles of today. Membership in the church was declining yearly, and in order to maintain their status in the world, congregants were very important to the Vatican.

Kathleen's father had joked with her about the confusion in canon law regarding the rule about eating meat on Fridays, which some believed one could simply break the rule then make a penance. She wondered if all those who had already gone to hell for eating meat on Friday before this review of the code, had been released to heaven following the Vatican's decision of the change.

As they entered the church, Kathleen made an extra dip in the holy water to cleanse herself. She paid close attention to the sermon today and said extra prayers following communion. She had always thought it was unfair that only the priest and assisting nun got to drink the wine. She could use some today, no doubt. Perhaps she and

Johnny would finally have a little time together tonight because he was not on call. Maybe on her walk home, she could also pick them up a bottle of wine.

For some reason, Kathleen left Mass feeling much better than she had in weeks, somewhat renewed and revived. She felt as though the crazy things that had been happening in her life were bearable. Father Paul had told a story of a man who continued to ask for a lighter cross to bear. When God granted his wish, he was directed to put down his own cross then enter a room where there were crosses in all different sizes, some very large and some small. Finally the man happened upon a small cross in the corner and chose that one. As he set about his way, God let him know that the cross he had selected was the very one that he had left at the door.

She had been down about her visions, her long hours at work, and of course, the baby, but she knew others had greater crosses to bear. The visions, although frightening at times, were elderly people who were probably set to pass away anyway. She knew realistically it was nothing she was causing and was grateful that at least she was able to help their families through the funeral and services. As for the job and its demands, it was what she had chosen for herself, and she knew that she was lucky to be able to work for herself in respectable business that had been part of her family for years. Many of her college friends were still unemployed, and she had very little tied up in student loans.

As for the baby, perhaps in many ways it was a blessing. She and Johnny really weren't ready for parenthood, and she did believe that more likely than not, there was something wrong with the baby. Kathleen was usually a positive person and looked to find the positive in all things. The sermon today helped her to refocus her attention on the positives in her life, and she was happy she had decided to go to church.

Kath set about on the errands she had planned to finish after church. She shopped around longer than she had anticipated because she was just glad to be out and about, taking her mind off her troubles. She choose a great Cab Franc to take to Johnny's tonight and decided that she would also pick up steaks and veggies for salad, which would be a great pairing with the wine. She wasn't much of a cook like her mother, but she could grill a steak easy enough and throw together a salad. No matter, because chances were good that Johnny would do the grilling, not her.

Of course, she ran into several people she knew who always threw out the worst funeral jokes. "How's business? Dead?" Then they would laugh as if they were the only one who had ever thought of such a thing. The worst joke—"If I ask you to do my hair, will I have to lie down?" The ladies in the pharmacy would get such a kick out of themselves Kath swore they had peed right in their Depends. They were probably at the drugstore to buy more right then.

While she was out, she texted Johnny to let him know she was bringing dinner and asked that he get a hold of her as soon as he leaves work. She was anxious to spend time with him, and even though she would not tell him about yesterday, just being close to him would make it all okay.

Dinner was fabulous, and Kathleen knew that the wine she had chosen was far greater quality than any Mass wine she missed earlier in the day. She and Johnny talked about lots of things, and Kathleen couldn't keep herself from asking how he felt about children. "Do you think we might have children someday? Is it something that you would want?"

"I think so, just one. My parents had a hard time raising me and my brothers, we were a lot of work. I think they are finally happy we all moved out. They seem to be in love again. But I would like at least one to carry on the family name."

"So you would prefer a boy—to carry on the name?"

Kath was a little disappointed, because she had always dreamed of a daughter herself. She was sure they would be happy with either. Who could predict anyway. They might decide to have more than one once they were settled and married.

"I guess so. I'd kill any man that ever touched my daughter."

"Oh, so it is all right for you to take advantage of another man's daughter, but no one better lay a hand on yours?" she jested.

"Speaking of taking advantage, why don't we sit in the living room and relax a little. The candles and wine were great while they lasted, but I need to be able to get closer to you."

His table was small because he really didn't have a dining room in his efficiency apartment. They had sat across from each other in the only two chairs that pulled up to the dark wooden table. It had a fold-down leaf, which allowed it to fit perfectly behind the couch in a small corner next to the very tiny kitchen. The apartment had one bedroom but was plenty big for just Johnny. He wasn't much of a pack rat and hated cleaning, so the smaller the place, the less he had to keep clean.

Kathleen knew there would be no hanky-panky tonight, but she figured she would broach the subject only if necessary. Just as they began to move to the couch, Kath's phone rang. It was her dad, so chances were she was going to have to go on a removal. Her mom and dad had also decided on dinner out, and Kathleen had promised if something came up, she would cover it. "Honey, we have a new call at Schuyler. Do you have a pen and paper?"

"Of course, Daddy, who is it?" She always kept her own notepad handy, having been taught by the best.

"It is an infant, full term but stillborn." He went on with all the details, name, parents' names, and phone contact. Kathleen wanted to coil up and throw the phone across the room, but it was not an option. *What are the chances of this happening right now?*

"Have you made contact with the family yet?"

"No, I was hoping you could. We are at the restaurant, and I really don't want to leave your mom waiting if possible."

No matter how bad she was feeling, she didn't want to disappoint her mother.

"I've got it, Dad. I will see you later."

She was going to have to go home, get the hearse, because her dad had the sedan, then grab the baby box and head out. First she thought she had better call the family and set up a time for arrangements. As she phoned them, she was planning to pawn the call off to her dad, but once she heard the voice of the man on the phone, she knew that she needed to meet with them herself. She wanted to be able to help them through this time because perhaps it would help her heal too. She set up arrangements for morning then invited Johnny to accompany her on the removal for moral support, of course, but she made him believe that it was just so they could continue their conversation.

They gathered the car and black box from the funeral home and headed for the morgue at Schuyler Hospital. All the way there, Kathleen was grateful that Johnny had come along. She just couldn't bear to think about doing this on her own. In fact, the family had wanted an embalming, and she was glad that she had such limited experience with infant embalming that she would have to leave that for her father. She wondered how the parents were feeling because they were so close to having a real living baby, almost any day and they had waited nine months in anticipation, but now nothing. Probably a nursery and other baby items were waiting at home. A far worse scenario than she had experienced, that was for sure.

They were in and out of the hospital in no time, and on the way back, she told Johnny that she was very tired, so she would drop him back at the apartment. It was true but not exactly why she wanted to go home; she actually just wanted to be alone so she could cry a little. He kissed her good night, and they made tentative plans for seeing each other the next day. "I am on call, but if things stay stagnant with the investigation, then I should be home at my regular time."

"I love you, Johnny. Thanks for being there for me tonight."

He really didn't know the extent to which her thank you reached but still accepted it and kissed her once again before she pulled away. She knew that she was lucky to have him and relished the day when they would have a baby of their own, planned, as it should be.

She reached the house and looped around the lot behind the funeral home to position herself to pull into the garage. She hated backing in, but when you had to leave for a removal in the middle of the night, it was much easier to just pull out and go. She hit the button on the garage door, put the car into reverse, and began her slow decent into the garage, watching every inch of the car in every mirror so as not to hit anything. As she had the car about halfway in, she checked again in her rearview mirror but slammed on her brakes as she noticed Mr. Carter standing in the middle of the garage. *How had he gotten in? Did he need something?*

She slammed the car into park and exited to figure out what he needed. As she began to walk toward the back, she hollered, "Mr. Carter, you scared me half to death, what can I do for you?" Now not even wondering how he got into the garage in the first place.

There was no response, and as she rounded the back of the hearse, she realized why. No-fucking-body was there. Her heart was pounding, and the fumes from the still-running hearse were bellowing through her nose, nearly making her light-headed. Was it the car fumes or her own foolish fears? She couldn't be sure, but she quickly got back in the hearse, parked it, and then returned the box to the prep table.

She left a note for her dad since she had decided she did not need to or want to be alone. She drove back to Johnny's in a flash then stayed all night in the safety of his arms.

It was just two days later when Mr. Carter passed away in his sleep at home. Perhaps he died of a broken heart over losing his wife, Kathleen assumed, as she recalled the tears she had evoked when she asked about whether or not he was married. His call came in on the morning of the burial services for the infant. It would be at least a day before the body was released because he was to have an autopsy due to his unattended death. Although he was elderly, he had no known health issues. She would be faced with another long, drawn-out embalming process, for likely no reason at all. The autopsy probably would show that he died of old age and a broken heart, nothing more. She wondered if a broken heart would be noted in the autopsy report. She wondered if a good pathologist would be able to tell.

CHAPTER 28

Since the baby burial was scheduled for today, Kath was not eager to climb out of bed. She had met with the Parker family a few days before to complete the arrangements for their baby. Mrs. Parker was released from the hospital the day after delivery, and she insisted on accompanying her husband for arrangements. They had named the baby Jeremiah and brought in a tiny blue outfit, blanket, and stuffed dog toy to be placed in his casket. They had decided on a private burial with family only and had purchased cemetery lots for themselves so they someday could be buried near Jeremiah. Not something they would likely use for years to come, but then again, you can't predict. They had certainly not predicted they would be buying cemetery lots instead of some new baby item for their now dead son.

Not only did Kath meet with the family, she was compelled to be the one to dress and casket the baby as well. It was her way to nurture this boy and ensure he was well taken care of before he was buried. Even though the parents decided not to view the baby, maybe because they had held him and taken pictures at the hospital, she still took time to make sure every detail of his clothing was perfect and wrapped him tightly in the blanket sent by his parents. Babies always looked like they were still alive, just asleep and still. His little hands curled up tight just like baby hands did.

She wished she could sprinkle magic dust on him and make him be alive. He looked so faultless that it was hard to imagine what had made this little guy not take one breath upon birth. His parents chose not to have an autopsy, which Kathleen was glad about due to its invasiveness. They had told Kathleen they believed that nature had done its job somehow, and he must have been flawed in some way, and she completely understood. Their faith helped them to be comforted that they would once again be together upon their own deaths.

The service was short with just the parents, grandparents, and Jeremiah's big sister. She must have been about two and was not quite sure whether to be sad, because all the other adults were, or to be her happy little self. Kathleen wondered if having another child would help ease their pain or if it would be a constant reminder of their failed attempt. She hoped it was going to ease their pain.

As she wrapped up at the cemetery, she waited a long while for the gravedigger to appear to close the grave. Thankfully because it was a small hole and an infant, the gravedigger agreed to make an exception and open the cemetery even though it was only mid-March. Usually it was April 1, no exceptions. Kathleen was pretty sure he was friends with the baby's grandfather. She had seen them talking behind the tool shed, and he slipped old Bill an envelope to thank him for his troubles.

When he finally arrived, the gravedigger gently shoveled the final layers of dirt on the tiny casket then replaced the sod that gave the effect of the ground never having been opened. Kathleen guessed they weren't as gentle with the covering of graves when no one was around or if it was an adult. At adult burials, the funeral director would leave once the lid was on the vault to let the gravedigger take care of business. In cases of a baby or urn, they had to wait it out because technically, someone could come along and take it, even though she doubted anyone would.

She placed the small funeral home issued marker she had made up on the grave, said a prayer for every sick baby, and then left a stronger woman.

As she drove away from the cemetery, she noticed it was lunchtime so decided she would swing by the ME's office to see if Johnny was able to leave for a few minutes. Something to eat would surely make her feel better, and she would get double pleasure if Johnny could join her.

She didn't often stop off at the office, but she was getting to know and like everyone there, and since she was not a nuisance, hanging out all the time, she was sure Johnny wouldn't get in trouble. The facility was so clean and sterile, had you not known it was a house of death, you'd never be the wiser. She stopped at the glass-enclosed reception booth and asked to see Johnny.

"I'll see if he is available."

She heard his name paged over the loudspeaker and was a little embarrassed she hadn't just called his cell like usual. The reception phone rang, and shortly after she hung up, Johnny appeared from the large metal door labeled Employees Only. "Hey, can you break out of this joint for a little lunch?"

"Give me five. We are just finishing up some paperwork after completing Mr. Carter's examination."

That was quick. She figured he wouldn't be released until at least tomorrow, but because of the crazy poisonings, must be they were clearing bodies much quicker to get samples to the labs. She was curious if Johnny knew anything more. She hadn't told him yet about her latest forewarning and seeing Mr. Carter in the garage. She would at lunch then dig for details about his death.

As it turned out, there was nothing that physically had stood out during Mr. Carter's autopsy, but they were still sending blood samples to the lab to test for the methanol poison. If that came back positive, there would have been at least seven poisoning deaths in the past fifteen months and possibly even more they were figuring, because they could not get permission for labs on everyone one who had died in every hospital in the area.

For a long time, the investigation had only been focused on Schuyler Hospital and Clear Rivers, but now they were beginning to believe this serial murderer was hitting more than just hospital patients. They had been extracting more and more samples for testing from home deaths too. There was no telling how many they had already missed or how long this had been going on before they discovered it.

Johnny seemed very withdrawn at lunch and less enthusiastic to share any details surrounding work, even with Kathleen's insistence. He just said there was nothing more they knew, but she still wondered if he was hiding something.

CHAPTER 29

Spring had come upon the DelGiorno family very quickly, and as Kathleen was approaching a year with the firm, Mr. DelGiorno was becoming more and more comfortable with her abilities. Even though it was spring burial season, he had decided to surprise his wife with a twenty-fifth anniversary gift and take her on a luxurious vacation to the Bahamas. It would be the first time they had been farther than a hundred miles from home in years. He could barely contain his anticipation to finally have the opportunity to give Jules the vacation she deserved. She was such a devoted wife and mother, and he loved everything about her. Not many women would have made it this far with his schedule and demands, but she never complained. She did escape to the lake often, and he never resented that because he knew that was what kept her around.

Back when Jules first found out about the vacation, she could barely speak. She had always wanted to travel, but due to the funeral home commitments, they were just unable to. She knew that Steve would someday take her on a dream vacation, but she had not expected it to be now. Once Jules learned of the trip, she immediately started to pack and plan for their departure.

Mr. DelGiorno had been organizing as many spring burials as he could to have them out of the way before he left, but he had also lined up Roger to help on a few while he was gone. It had been a rather mild winter, so a few cemeteries had stayed open into January, and as he checked his list, he found they had just twenty-one burials to make up. Not too bad, but enough. Often they would try to schedule two or more in a day in the same cemetery, which would be much easier with Kathleen now working.

It was time to go to the vault to pick up their burial of the day, so he rounded up Kathleen and the paperwork he needed, a burial permit and check for the cemetery, then retreated to the hearse. They would first have to stop at the holding vault. Although they closed, many cemeteries had no place to store the bodies until spring, so for a fee, other cemeteries that had holding vaults would let the funeral homes store caskets there. They were headed to Hope vault, then on to the rural Old Valley Cemetery about five miles out of town.

The caretaker had to meet them at the cemetery to unlock the vault door, and as usual, he was on time, waiting for them. He was a reliable old chap and had been caring for the cemetery ever since Mr. DelGiorno could remember.

The holding vault was actually an old chapel where services used to be held before burials. This was before they had fancy equipment and fake grass to cover the gaping hole in the ground. Now that they could make the graveside look presentable, people preferred to go straight to the grave if for no other reason but in hopes of ever finding it again. Depending on the size of the cemetery, it was not very easy to find a grave without a map or photographic memory.

The holding vault was stable but very run-down. The only remnants that indicated it was previously a chapel were the large arched stained glass windows. There were some signs of colored glass still in them, but on the outside, they had been boarded up with plywood to cover the holes. It was dusty and drab but served its purpose. No worse than the dark underground cave each would soon be entrusted to for eternity.

They loaded Mr. Oliver in the hearse then headed in the direction of Old Valley. As they got closer, the road became windier, and from somewhere, Mr. DelGiorno could hear water swaying back and forth. Maybe the gas tank was sloshing, he reasoned, although he had not noticed it ever before.

Around the next corner the sound was even louder and by then Kathleen could also hear the sloshing noise her father was trying to figure out. Water swishing and hitting something then swishing back. Next corner the same. Mr. Oliver, Steve recalled, was a large man who had been getting chemo for his lung cancer. He, as it would turn out, had not been one to hold his embalming. It happened occasionally, especially when people died of certain diseases or with lots of fluid already in their tissue.

Embalming, although some would never guess, was not meant as an ultimate preservation like in ancient Egypt but rather a disinfectant and preservation to get through services. Usually, except due to spring burial, bodies were interred quick enough so that no one would be the wiser. Now, although not spoken, both Kathleen and her dad were wishing this had been one corpse that had not been held over.

The sound of the sloshing nearly made Kathleen sick, and Mr. DelGiorno kept his usual calm, as if to say, "This happens all the time"—it didn't. The family would be meeting them at the cemetery, and even though they had arranged pallbearers, there was no way they would be touching this casket. Mr. DelGiorno sped up a little and was relieved when he turned the corner to see that no one had arrived at the cemetery yet.

They backed right up to the grave and carefully slid the casket from the hearse to the bier with as little sway as possible, just in time for the first car to arrive. Although it was a metal unit with a fail-safe liner, nobody was eager to test its reliability today. Nothing appeared to be amiss, but to be safe, Mr. DelGiorno still had the vault man lower the casket a couple inches below the fake green grass that covered the casket-lowering device.

Instead of carrying the casket, Mr. DelGiorno immediately instructed the pallbearers to split three to each side to stand guard at the casket. He acted as if this was usual protocol for spring burials. The service couldn't have been over quick enough for him. They still had fifteen spring burials to go after this, and Mr. DelGiorno prayed this would be their first and only problem going forward.

CHAPTER 30

B y the time the DelGiornos were ready to leave for vacation, they had just six spring burials left, and most were scheduled after he returned. They were easy to schedule ahead, but then it required them to plan any new at-need calls around the burials. Steve figured if he had them all ready before he left, he could relax with no worries until he returned. Kathleen would have to take care of the two this week, but Roger was coming over as needed to help out. In fact, of the two burials, one was a cremation, so Kathleen would probably not even need Roger to help on that one. Either way, Mr. DelGiorno was confident the two of them could handle it.

The funeral home had been quiet since her parents had left, and it was somewhat of a relief for Kathleen. That was until the phone rang. It was the Gunderman family, who were scheduled to bury their mother in a couple of days. She had passed away in November, just after the cemetery closed. Mrs. Gunderman had two daughters, and this was her sane daughter warning Kathleen about her sister's insistence to view the body after five months in the winter vault. It had been an odd service that included a professional photographer to take pictures of the deceased in the casket.

Kathleen was very much flabbergasted when she arrived at the calling hours months ago to stand the door and there was a professional photographer on a stepladder, hovering over the casket, taking a variety of shots. That should have been a clue to the extended grief that was now presenting itself. Insisting on opening the casket months later was just not normal.

Kath really just wanted to tell them to pull out the photo album as it would make for a more pleasant viewing, she imagined, especially after the recent episode in dealing with a body that had not preserved well.

Kathleen and the daughter had a good conversation, and both agreed that it was not a good idea to reopen the casket, simply because there was just no telling what could be on the inside. They had a good relationship, and this daughter had even bought her a gift after her mother's funeral. A glass apple that Kath still kept on her dresser. She had only received a gratuity, or rather a thank-you gift, from three other families in her life. In addition to the squash pie, one was a one-hundred-dollar bill, almost as a tip, which was a little awkward, the other a hand-crocheted pair of slippers that Kathleen still wore every night even though they were threadbare. They reminded her of the blankets and ponchos her grandma used to make for the family. She had just one left that still lay on the end of her bed. A piece her grandmother was so discouraged about she nearly ripped apart, but Kath told her it was perfect, and she finally finished it.

During their conversation, Kathleen politely conveyed her concerns in layman's terms and felt confident that her explanation would help to appease the other daughter once her sister had explained everything. The daughter was in agreement, and she also felt that her sister was a bit disturbed to want to go through with it. Forget about the fact that the family had still not paid their seven-thousand-dollar bill after five months either, but a funeral home was not allowed to withhold burial or any other services for lack of payment. Not a very fair rule.

It wasn't very often that families didn't pay, but at times, estates were held up for longer than planned, which delayed payment. There were few instances, of course, that people just simply did not pay at all. One account that particularly troubled her father was with a family who had lost their son in an accidental drowning in the local river. He had played there often and misjudged the strength of the river that day. The family did not have much money and had lots of kids, so Kathleen's father was generous in keeping the funeral costs affordable. Some community members had even held a benefit to offset funeral costs. Unfortunately, the money was turned over to the family, and instead of paying off the funeral home, they ironically chose to purchase a brand-new pool instead.

As she hung up the phone with Mrs. Gunderman's sane daughter, Kath had no worries that she could convince her sister to forego the viewing. Unfortunately, the phone call Kathleen received the following day proved her to be wrong. The daughter requesting the viewing had not taken her sister's recommendations well and proceeded to call the State Health Department Bureau of Funeral Directing. In turn, Ms. Orwitchie, current head of the department, felt she needed to advocate for the family. From the other end of the line, she promptly scolded Kathleen for her denial, so she called it, of a spring viewing. Kathleen explained that she had not denied the viewing, simply advised against it, which was part of the guidance she had the duty to provide to *her* families. Ms. Orwitchie did not agree but Kathleen continued that if she felt it was a safe bet, perhaps she would like to come down and risk her own health to open it for the family. That did not go over well, and therefore the conversation was cut short with a warning from Ms. Orwitchie to allow the viewing.

"Uuuggghh! What a bitch!" Kathleen shouted as she hung up the phone, even though no one was there to listen. Kathleen proceeded to call the daughter she had been discussing the arrangements with, and they agreed that Kathleen would first open the casket alone to avoid any surprises.

Kathleen wished her dad was there to deal with this. She did not need to be on the hot seat with the state, since she was just over a month away from being fully licensed. She also felt her dad might be better able to reason with this family. She would have to handle it, and she assured herself everything would turn out just fine, then she picked up the phone to call Roger for a little advice. "Hey, Rog, your favorite funeral director here," she declared. "I need your help."

"What's up, got a live one?"

"As a matter of fact, it is a live one, actually, two that are giving me troubles."

She went on to explain the situation and gave him all the details about the crazy daughter and the wrath of Ms. Orwitchie. She confirmed she needed some moral and professional support the next day at the vault as she planned to check out the situation a day in advance. She enlightened Roger about the "slosher" they buried a week or so ago and told him that she definitely wouldn't know what to do if they found Mrs. Gunderman in a similar condition.

"I can be there at ten. Will that work for you? I've bailed your dad out of enough strange predicaments before, and I'll have your back too." He laughed.

"Sounds great," she replied in a grateful voice. "I'll arrange for the vault to be opened, and I'll bring the gloves, nose plugs, and cosmetics, just in case."

He must have still sensed the worry in her voice because Roger immediately started in on a story of a mishap he and Steve had encountered years ago. She guessed mainly to help ease her mind that every funeral director has a bad day.

He went on to tell her about a burial he and her father were in charge of a long time ago. It was actually a call that generated from Roger's family funeral home, but they had called her dad to help because they were busy with several other calls that day. He recalled that the family name was Finch but couldn't be sure of the first name. Regardless, he went on to tell about their arrival in a very rural, unkempt, swampy cemetery in Northern, Pennsylvania. The boys were both greenbacks to the profession, but it should have been an easy drop-and-go service. The family had followed along in a trail of about twenty vehicles behind the hearse from the funeral home for the sixty-mile trek.

He described in detail how the day was hot and muggy, and even with the long dry summer, the place had been so nasty that the goo clung to their shoes like honey on bread. The family members began to trudge toward the cemetery tent to participate in the last rights of Mr. Finch. As the cemetery keeper approached them, he appeared just as unkempt as the cemetery grounds and wore several layers of smelly clothes and a dusty Russian-style hat. Based on his appearance and conversation they had, Roger distinctly remembered this man's mind being somewhere between La-La Land and Clueless town.

Just as Steve was approaching the grave keeper to make small talk and pass along the grave opening check, an older lady from the family jumped in the caretaker's face, screaming uncontrollably. Screams that had to be heard lest believed, so Mr. DelGiorno, the professional that he was, walked over to see if he could help.

A move he likely regretted because as he approached, he realized the problem was that the cemetery keeper had opened the wrong grave. He was walking right into a hornet's nest. The grave that was opened happened to be the screaming lady's grave. Now she truly believed she was cursed to be the next to die. With all the commotion, the entire family began to argue followed by the old lady screaming that "everything he did turned to shit!"

While Steve hoped it wouldn't get any worse, he saw Roger, the pallbearers, and the casket traipsing through the mud toward the grave that was clearly not the right final resting place for Mr. Finch. All of a sudden, out of pure desperation and in hopes of saving his own ass, the cemetery keeper whipped off his dusty old hat and pointed at Steve and declared, "It is *his* fault. He is supposed to mark the grave."

Although that was the furthest thing from the truth, the old man thought it was the only way he could save himself and turned on his muddy shoes and stormed off. As Roger closed in on the arguments, he quickly realized what the problem was, so he promptly turned the pallbearers about-face and, as calmly as could be, asked the family to join him at the hearse for a committal service. Easily explaining that he and Steve would return Mr. Finch to the cemetery on Monday to ensure the burial took place.

"Pulling out that day, Kathleen, I swore your dad was ready to quit the business, but before long, we were laughing and reminiscing about this story and still do today. Don't worry, everything will turn out fine. Look at the mess I got your dad out of due to my utter calmness."

As she hung up the phone, she was relieved that at least if her dad couldn't be there, she would have a competent and experienced funeral director if things turned out bad. She was ready to go head to head with Ms. Orwitchie if she found anything less than pleasant to share with the Gunderman family.

CHAPTER 31

It turned out that Mrs. Gunderman was in great shape when Roger and she opened the casket the next day. Kathleen imagined she could put the professional photos next to Mrs. Gunderman, and one would guess they were taken the same day. There was a slight odor, nothing a quick spritz of air freshener couldn't mask just before the family arrived. The only discoloration was due to the flowers that had been left in her hands. They had dried up and molded, so they removed them and wiped off the hands, and she looked great. All that worry for nothing, but Kathleen still felt that she had been correct in suggesting that they rethink their choice in the first place. They had lucked out this time, but she certainly didn't want to start a trend for future spring burials. Hopefully the family wouldn't share their idea with others. Kathleen thanked Roger as they finished up and went to their cars. "Ah hell, I wouldn't have missed it for the world. I was curious what we might find. Was this your dad's handiwork or yours?" he inquired.

"Well, as a matter of fact, this particular case was a team effort. We do superior embalming work, so truly I had no doubt we would find this body in perfect condition," she confidently retorted.

"Okay, short stuff, if that is what you want to believe, but your call yesterday seemed pretty desperate. I am just glad I was here to help," he bragged.

She smiled as she loaded herself back into the Cadillac and tooted the horn as she pulled away. She laughed to herself at Roger's comebacks. He was always a smart-ass and so proved himself to be one again today. She looked up to Roger as a second father and was pleased that he had been more than willing to help her out.

When Kathleen returned to the funeral home, she called the daughters to confirm the viewing then decided she needed to take a break from her work for a while. She then called Johnny in hopes of making dinner plans. She figured she could try to cook tonight, being that the house was empty, and she could perhaps attempt to create something edible. Johnny would be available around six o'clock, so she logged onto her computer to find some recipes online then ran off to the store to gather her ingredients.

She returned from the store a little skeptical about whether or not she could actually pull off what she had set out to do, but after the burst of confidence she experienced earlier in the day about her embalming skills, she had to believe she could easily make a meal of fettuccini with grilled chicken and shrimp.

She put the wine she had bought in the fridge to chill then set about her task. By the time she finished her prep, she was amazed at the mess she had made but thankful that her mom wasn't there to see it and that Johnny wouldn't be there for a couple more hours.

With dinner nearly prepared, her only obstacle was to avoid a funeral call, which she knew she had very little control over, but still prayed it wouldn't happen.

As she heard Johnny pull up, she could hardly believe how perfect her timing was. She had just finished the homemade Alfredo sauce and was mixing the noodles and meat with it. The meal would be ready to serve, hot as planned, as he walked in the door. She almost felt like June Cleaver awaiting Ward. She had watched reruns of *Leave it to Beaver* on Nick at Night when she was younger but had always hated the idea of being a housewife. Tonight, however, she found the role fulfilling.

Johnny entered, and Kathleen could tell right away there must be something weighing on his mind. He still tried to pretend nothing was wrong and beamed a bright white smile at her to show his appreciation for what smelled like a delicious feast. "I can't wait to dig in. I didn't get a lunch break today. What's on the menu?"

"Well, sir, have a seat, and your server will be with you shortly," she jested.

As he sat down, she immediately poured him a tall glass of Riesling, and he took a long hard swig. She poured herself a glass and went to retrieve two heaping plates of her masterpiece. She hoped he would enjoy it not just because he was starving but because she wanted it to be appetizing too.

She waited for Johnny's first bite, and as he began to chew, he made a clenching motion toward his throat and a gagging noise. "This is the most . . ." he hesitated for a long while with a look of disgust on his face, "delicious meal I have had in a long time. Even beats my mother's," he concluded with a smile.

Kathleen wanted to believe that he was being absolutely honest but really didn't care because he was so convincing she felt special on many levels. Perhaps she would do a little more cooking to prepare for her role as his wife. She wanted to please him and knew the best way to a man's heart was through his stomach.

She dug in and was pleased with the results. It was pure delight on the palette. The wine made the food even more enjoyable, and before they even finished their plates, they had almost polished off the full bottle. Johnny was not sipping his wine but rather gulping tonight, which confirmed her suspicion that there might be something wrong. Once the meal was finished and they were settled in to relax, she would find out about his day. She didn't want to ruin the meal if it was something he did not want to talk about.

Before long, they had cleaned up from dinner and were finally able to go up to the sitting room to chill. Kathleen was so full she almost regretted having made such a delicious dinner. She felt as if she might puke any minute. She had gotten her favorite peanut butter chocolate pie from the market but knew that she would need some time before eating that. She didn't even offer it.

For a short time, they made small talk, Kathleen describing her episode with the Gunderman family and how today she was greatly relieved by the outcome. Kathleen also expressed her excitement about her parents' return. It was only a few more days before her parents were to get home, and she commented on how she was looking forward to finding out every detail about their trip, one her mother so much deserved.

Their cell phone service would not work on the island, so her parents had not been able to make contact since they left the airport on the coast of North Carolina. She was sure the trip was more than either could have imagined. If it turned out to be a great spot, she and Johnny had discussed that perhaps they would choose it for their upcoming honeymoon destination.

As Johnny began to tell of his uneventful day, she still sensed that he was holding something from her. She dug deeper and insisted she could read him like a book, flashing her eyes at him to plead for disclosure.

He reached out for her hand and began with the all-too-annoying, "I have something to tell you, but I need you to be calm and not get upset." He looked at her for reassurance, and she tried her best to present a look to confirm she was confident that she could handle whatever was coming her way.

A million thoughts flooded her mind, and although only seconds had passed, the anticipation was killing her. *Was he calling off the engagement, had he fallen in love with the receptionist at work, worse, was he gay?* She quickly removed that thought because he was too damn sexy to be smokin' the bologna pony.

"Kathleen." He paused for what seemed like an eternity. "It has to do with your father. I need you to keep this in strict confidence because I could very easily lose my job."

"I will!" she quickly responded, sensing some relief that it wasn't going to be the breakup speech but in turn feeling a bit of panic because it involved her father.

"You need to know that there is no absolute evidence, just circumstances that have led our investigation of the recent poisonings to your father. Of the current deaths, the only thing the victims have in common is that they were indeed poisoned and that they all were buried at his funeral home."

He was right, what the hell did that prove? She moved from anger to surprise and then back to anger in a flash.

Defensively she replied, "Well, who were they, which calls, maybe I can shed some light on this?"

He went down the list, and eerily with almost every name he ticked off his list, the visions played back in her head. Nearly every person Jonny had just named matched up perfectly with the people Kathleen had seen in her premonitions. The hair stood up on her neck, and the previous full feeling in her stomach now turned sour, as if she really was going to upchuck right then and there. Before she could even think about how ridiculous it would sound, she blurted out, "Those are the ones in my visions, the people I saw before their deaths. What could this mean?"

She was now teetering between anxiety about what she had seen, and perhaps even done to cause these deaths, back to the anger she first felt toward Johnny for even suggesting that her father might be involved. *How dare he?* Johnny knew her father well, and he surely understood her dad was nothing but dedicated to his profession. Her dad certainly could not be involved, but more puzzling was that she had predicted each of these deaths. Johnny sensed the anxiety in her face. "Kathleen, your apparitions could not have caused these people's death, let alone have poisoned them," he reassured her. "It is not possible, and you know it."

He continued to sense her doubt and confusion as he searched for the right thing to say.

"Listen, I will keep you up to date with the information that is being gathered, but in the meantime, you cannot tell anyone. I doubt that anything will come about in regards to your dad. I just felt like I needed to tell you about the connection. It is a strange coincidence, but very unlikely that he would do such a thing. We both know that."

She was beginning to feel a bit more at peace by his reassuring words. She trusted that he would not withhold information and, if possible, would stick up for her father's good name. They ended the night wrapped in each other's arms, both wondering silently where this whole thing would lead. When they both finally crashed into deep sleep, mentally drained, neither awoke until the next morning.

CHAPTER 32

The next day, Kathleen and Johnny set out to their jobs with the goal of ensuring they served with honor any person they had been entrusted. Kathleen finished up the Gunderman burial with everyone leaving happy and returned to the funeral home to prepare for another spring burial. This one would be easier to plan and prepare for because it was not a full burial but rather a cremation inurnment. Yet she knew that this burial would be emotional because it was for a family friend.

This call was for the grandmother of a close childhood friend, Heather. Mrs. Houson had passed away earlier in the year and had been cremated but could not be buried because the cemetery was closed. Kathleen looked forward to seeing the family again tomorrow. It would be a nice break from the demanding family she had worked with today.

When Mrs. Houson had passed away, even though she lived over twenty miles away, they had wanted the DelGiornos to handle it at their firm. It was easy since it was a direct cremation. Following the cremation, there was a church service in her hometown. This didn't require the use of a funeral home, making the call easy to arrange in Watkins Glen then carry out in Bath. The burial would also take place in Bath, and Kathleen looked forward to getting away from the funeral home for a couple of hours.

She called to confirm the cemetery opening then decided she had better get an inventory of prep room supplies, as it had been a while since she had ordered, and they surely would need something soon. Kathleen loved keeping things organized and had designed an ongoing checklist to make ordering easier when she returned from college. She grabbed the form from the file then snapped it on the clipboard and went off to complete her task.

As she passed through to the prep room, she glanced over at the box of long-forgotten body parts and reminded herself that she must get on that task of attempting to notify the families. A sense of guilt almost made her regret she had even gone to the basement in the first place. She would take care of it, she reassured herself, as soon as these last few spring burials were done.

She returned to studying her inventory list and started ticking off items that needed to be ordered. She worked her way through the cupboards and drawers of cosmetics and personal protection equipment then grabbed the key to the embalming fluid case. She flipped open the lock and, once inside, saw that her prediction was spot on. The cupboard was nearly bare, and she felt a little like Old Mother Hubbard in need of a bone.

She carefully counted each container, checking against the previous order on the list to see how much of each they had used since the last order. While her dad liked to be sure they had enough in stock, it was very expensive, so he did not like to order more than they needed at one time. Arterial fluid, softener, tint, and cavity fluid were all getting low. As she pulled her hand from the cupboard, she accidently knocked a few bottles of the cavity fluid, Cav-all, to the ground.

Kathleen reached down to retrieve the bottles, which were now discombobulated in all directions, some heads up and some heads down. Thankfully, none had sprung open. She would have surely had to evacuate the room because of its potent smell and fumes that carried like a dandelion in the wind.

She began to rearrange them neatly on the shelf, but as she placed the final bottle, a word stood out to her like a red pimple on a bare white butt. Ingredients: formaldehyde and *methanol.*

The poison Johnny had spoken about months ago. It had never occurred to her that it was in the cavity fluid. She must have learned about it in mortuary school, but those were the things easily forgotten because as long as the product worked, who really cared what was in it?

Not being very science minded, she had been glad during college that her coursework at mortuary school was concentrated only on what one needed to know to be a funeral director. She had taken chemistry, anatomy, and microbiology, but each course was designed to teach what they needed to know for the business of embalming, not to become a scholarly scientist. The coursework extensively studied body anatomy but no physiology because that pertained to the living. For sure, they had learned the chemical elements of formaldehyde and ingredients of the embalming chemicals that she used, but it was not something that she had to remember to be a funeral director.

The chemicals were neatly packaged with proper amounts for an average human to be embalmed, and if someone knew the fluid-water ratio, that was probably enough. She didn't once think about the ingredients in those bottles after she had passed her National Board Exam and really didn't need to.

Without a doubt, the coroner's office and other investigators had researched that this poison was an element in cavity fluid, which had probably led them to look closer at the funeral profession and ultimately her father. But there were plenty of funeral directors with access to this very same chemical. There had to be other coincidences. Maybe someone else was committing the murders to make it look like her father; a setup by a competitor seemed logical to her. Much more logical than her own father being involved.

She finished up her inventory, locked the cupboard, and returned to the office a little more convinced her dad could be involved, but she insisted to herself she was not going to jump the gun. There had to be an explanation, and when her dad returned, she would feel him out, carefully so as not to let on that there was an investigation. That could jeopardize Johnny's job. She felt a little torn between being faithful to her promise to Johnny or to protect her father's reputation.

Dodge chemical company was listed in the rolodex, and she carefully flipped through so she could phone in her inventory order. She neatly wrote the number at the top of the inventory list to save time when she ordered next. She always looked for ways to save steps. As she placed the order, they requested the customer number, one thing she always forgot to look up ahead of time. She made a mental note to add these two items to the master order form the next time she printed one. She pulled open the desk file drawer and grabbed the invoice folder. The customer number was listed at the top of the old packing lists, and it was the only place she knew to find it.

Order complete. She relished in her accomplishments of the day then began to tidy up the desk and get ready to call it a day. She filed all the finished spring burial folders that had been piled high on the desk in the tall wooden file drawers, organized by year and date of death. Her father had purchased a matching wooden desk, filing cabinet, and urn display cabinet just a few years back to make the office homier. As she plopped back in the chair of the large desk, she tidied up the tape dispenser and stapler and returned the few pens that were scattered back into the cup. She opened the drawer to slide the invoice folder back into its place. As she fanned her fingers over the files to find its spot, a folder jumped out at her; it was red, and she recalled that her father had been reading from a red folder months ago, and how as she approached the office, he had quickly put it away.

No one here to catch her now. As part owner, there shouldn't be any secrets, she reasoned. Still, somewhat reluctantly, she pulled out the folder and was quite intrigued by what its contents might be. As she peeled back the cover, a list appeared. As she began to scan the list of about fifty names top to bottom, there were a few names she recognized but did not make any connection to what the list meant.

Beside each name was a date of death, some going back over ten years, and a checkmark under a column labeled Paid. As she ruffled more papers, she came across a bankbook labeled Vacation Fund, with deposits matching a day or two before each death date listed. A large withdraw was also there a few days before her parents' vacation.

She chuckled about how sneaky her dad was to have hidden money from her mother so that he could surprise her. That was the true love that she hoped she and Johnny would continue to have for years to come, like her parents. Her dad cherished the ground Jules walked on, and if Johnny was half as dedicated to her as her dad to her mom, she would never feel unloved.

She continued to read down the list, trying to make sense of it, and as the death dates came closer to the present, some of the names became familiar. She recognized the name of Mrs. Carter. She was the wife of Mr. Carter, who had recently been in one of Kathleen's premonitions. She continued reading the names one by one, and as she edged toward the end of the list, each name became eerily familiar.

Angela Dunfee
Theodore Thomas
Marion Updike
Jennifer Delabarto
Jack O'Brien
Joseph Carter—the final name that appeared on the list.

All at once, she realized what this fucking list was. This was a list of victims. Many had matched perfectly with the names Johnny had recited to her last night because they were part of the investigation. The last six were also the ones she had seen, the ones she was warned about. Had there been something she could have done? Would there have been something she would have done?

Her mind raced, looking for justification for her dad's list. Well, she reasoned, the ones she knew were either all terminally ill or at the very least elderly. Her mind twisted back to horror. Christ, was he some type of sick serial murderer character? If so, then why was he being paid to put these people out of their misery? A hit man? Mob boss? Were people paying him to get rid of their elderly families so they could collect an inheritance?

She suddenly felt the urge to vomit, but instead of heading toward the bathroom, instinct took her directly to the hearse, so she could get the hell out of there. She had no idea where she was going but knew she wanted out. The papers were left scattered on the desk, but she did not even care at this point.

Who would be next? Would she see them and be able to stop it? When nothing appeared in the rearview mirror, she turned over the engine, opened the garage door, and then whipped out of there with such speed the hearse rocked back and forth. This time she couldn't keep her eyes off the mirror, even though recently she had been avoiding it at all costs. Still nothing. Maybe she was trying too hard.

She ended up at Johnny's house, not caring at all that she had just parked a hearse at his front stoop, which would no doubt cause uproar in the neighborhood. She barely made it in the door when she fell into his arms, sobbing uncontrollably. It took her nearly fifteen minutes before she could even begin to gain her composure and explain what she had found. She needed to tell him everything. "Promise me you won't tell just yet. I need a day or two to gather my thoughts, tell my mom. Fuck! I don't want him arrested at the airport on their arrival home. I need to clarify this with him first. Promise me, please," she pleaded.

"Kathleen, what the hell are you talking about?" he scolded and then reverted to a more thoughtful voice. "I promise, we will get through this together. I promise. What is it?"

The story flooded out almost as if it were a prepared speech, but much faster than an experienced public speaker. She poured over every detail, clarifying both to herself and Johnny the events that looked all too suspicious for her father to be innocent. It was more than just a confession but also a realization of how serious this might be. Regardless, a weight had been lifted just blurting it all out and knowing that she could trust Johnny with her secret.

By the time she left Johnny's, it was late at night, and she had barely noticed how fast time had passed or that she had never brought her phone. Her mind went quickly back to her duties to DelGiorno Funeral Home. She hoped she hadn't missed a call. No matter what her father had done, this business was well respected in the community, and no matter what might come of it, she still wanted their families to be well taken care of.

As soon as she returned home, she checked her phone and was relieved the only call she had missed was a girlfriend. Thankfully not a death call. She tossed and turned all night long, wondering if this nightmare would end better than she expected. She kept running scenarios through her mind, imagining her father would have such a silly explanation for what had happened. That they would laugh for years about her perceived guilt once everything was out in the open.

She finally fell asleep just hours before she had to get back up to run Mrs. Houson's burial. At least she would have something to take her mind off her father's predicament for a little while. She looked forward to seeing her old friend too.

As she awoke, she reminded herself that her parents would be home late tomorrow. She would speak privately to her dad about the file when the timing was right, but she knew it would have to be sooner than later. She moved quickly to get ready, planning her day as she dressed, pretending as best as she could that nothing was amiss. It would be a good day to call back her girlfriend Mimi, who had called last evening. They had intended to get together for months now, and Kathleen wanted to ask her to be in the wedding. If she made plans with her and discussed the wedding, she could pull herself away from the misery she was experiencing now.

She cranked the music on the way to the burial and switched stations when any song came on that was not upbeat and peppy. Mrs. Houson was riding along shotgun in her urn. Kathleen was looking forward to seeing Heather and thought maybe they could catch up over a cup of coffee after the service. Of course, because she wanted to spend time with Heather, but also so that she could keep her mind off the impending doom.

She entered the cemetery slowly and then glanced at her directions that were given by the cemetery keeper. When there was no vault or vault truck to spot on the way in, finding a lot in the cemetery was worse than finding a needle in a haystack, especially because there was also no tent to guide her to the grave.

The family arrived just shortly after Kathleen, but she had already set up a small stand and some fake grass to cover the rawness of the bare ground and hole beneath. As they piled out, just the five of them, Deb, her husband, and their two grown children, along with Deb's brother, Sean, they all began to hug as it had been months since they had seen Kathleen. Actually, this was the shortest time between their visits ever.

Heather and her family did not live here but would visit almost every summer at the lake. They had lived in several places around the country because her dad was an executive with Frito-Lay. They currently lived in Texas, which was a long way from New York, so their visits had become even less frequent. Besides, Heather was now grown up and finishing college. The families had kept in touch because Deb and Jules were high school friends. It was odd that they both grew up in Syracuse, but Deb's mother had moved so close to where Jules's family had ended up, making it possible for them to visit when Deb came home.

Kathleen recalled the sweet anticipation of knowing that Heather would be coming to visit each summer. She would count down the months, weeks, then days. They had known each other since they were babies and would pick up each summer like they had never been separated. They were best friends. When Heather came, it meant trips to the lake and their first tries at water skiing. Kathleen always looked forward to spending a little time at Mrs. Houson's house too. Heather and her family always stayed at her grandmother's, and so many memories were made right in that house.

Croquet in the backyard. Finding ways to annoy her uncle Sean, who had never moved away because he had some mental issues, but they did not know that back then; maybe they would have been nicer. Singing Barry Manilow's "Mandy" on the stairs, which served as their stage, as Mrs. Houson played the organ below them. Listening intently to Heather once again tell the tale about how she was born with six fingers with all of us carefully examining the scars that ran down her pinky all the way to her wrist on each hand.

Kathleen loved Mrs. Houson's house too. Her favorite features were the swinging arched door to the dining room and the fluffy pink pillows on the window seat in the same room that housed the organ. Mrs. Houson was an artist and had painted a mural on the wall with Heather, her mother, her stepdad, and their dog. Then, when Heather's little brother came along, Grandma had added little David to the picture. Kathleen remembered studying that picture every time she visited. She always thought about how much Heather's grandmother must have loved them to paint their pictures right on her wall. A picture that was surely gone since they had sold the house just a few months ago.

The minister arrived as scheduled, and the burial prayers for Mrs. Houson began. Kathleen was surprised by her inability to contain her sorrow. She wept hard that day not only for Mrs. Houson but also it was grief for the passing youth and friendship. She knew that she and Heather probably would never see each other again, and the once-felt anticipation you get as a child when waiting for someone or something special would not be felt again. With Heather's grandmother gone, there was nothing at all to bring them back to New York. Although Kathleen always pretended that Heather came just to visit her, that was not really the case. Being older now, she knew that. Kathleen grieved in knowing that this may very well be the last time she will see any of them, a chapter in her life ending.

She cried harder than anyone there, and before long, all were consoling her instead of the other way around. It was somewhat ironic for her but a rite of passage as well. Learning that sometimes it was okay to be the griever, the one who let go, who was allowed to show emotion. Kathleen was feeling much better having cleansed her soul. After having coffee and sharing memories with Heather following the burial, she had nearly forgotten that she had more grief to face in the near future when she confronted her dad.

CHAPTER 33

The anticipated arrival of Kathleen's parents was bittersweet. She couldn't wait to see them and hear about their trip, but the dread about having a discussion with her father was weighing very heavily upon her. As the taxi brought them up the drive, she ran out to greet them and help with their luggage. It took everything she had to not let her pending conversation with her dad ruin her mother's opportunity to tell all about their trip.

Jules went on for hours and scanned through the digital photos they had taken, giving every detail of their adventures. Her eyes lit up like Kathleen had never seen before, and already Jules was planning where they would go on their next vacation. Kathleen was thrilled that her mother had gotten the opportunity to go on a very well deserved vacation with her father and that they both had had such a great time.

At least for the few hours while they discussed the trip, it kept Kathleen's mind from the inevitable discussion she needed to have with her father.

Once her mother was busy unpacking and getting herself reorganized and reoriented with being home, Kathleen went in search of her father. He had talked about his favorite parts of the trip, but had finished with all he had to say about it long before Jules. He was sitting in the office, and as she turned the corner, she couldn't help but admire his dedication to his work and the families he served. She was grateful she had remembered to put the red folder away after she had left in such a rush two days ago. She so desired that this mess would go away or that his side of the story would make everything turn out fine.

"Dad, you sure made Mom happy with that vacation. She couldn't stop talking about all the great things you did. Thank you for taking such good care of her."

Kathleen meant what she said, and even knowing that soon she might know of a darker side of her father, she loved him dearly.

"I couldn't love her more, Kathleen. It means a lot to me to know that I have someone I can trust to take care of the business so that I could finally give her what she had waited so long for. She has sacrificed a lot to be married to a funeral director all these years."

Kathleen just savored the moment, knowing that once she made her discovery known that their whole world would be turned upside down. In her eyes, at least, a world that had been so perfect all her life. She didn't even know what was going to happen to her father if what she believed was actually true. They may even lose the funeral home, which would be terrible for all of them, but then again, if her dad was a murderer and somehow was paid, then maybe their family didn't deserve to keep the funeral home either. She knew in a few short minutes, her family would be forever changed. Her mother would be devastated for sure, no matter what the outcome.

"You look like something is on your mind, Kath, what is it?" he asked in his fatherly way.

He always could tell when something was bothering Kathleen. They were very close and so much alike it was almost as if he had a sixth sense about her feelings. She wavered a long while before she finally spoke, not sure if she wanted to find out the truth. Knowing that once she opened the floodgate, she could never turn back.

She started with the details of the investigation and could immediately tell that her dad was surprised that one was even underway. At first he acted as any concerned person would who had heard the news, but Kathleen could sense his uneasiness. Finally she just blurted it out. "Dad, they're investigating funeral homes, and your name has been mentioned." Her words were stammering out of her mouth rapidly. "I found your red folder and somehow the last six names on your list are the same people who have been poisoned. Tell me that your list has nothing to do with this, Daddy! Please!"

He was precise with his movements even though they were few, and she could tell he had something to say but was contemplating very carefully how he should respond. He oddly straightened things on the desk as a distracter then ran his fingers through his peppery-gray hair. It had become more peppered since Kathleen had returned from school—she just noticed. Their eyes stared at one another, and the bond that made them family held strong. Kathleen could not wait any longer.

"Dad, answer me! You don't understand, there is more. Each of the most recent poisonings you have been involved with all came to me in visions. I saw them before they died. What if they were asking for help, telling that they did not want you to come? I need to know what the fuck is going on."

A rush of emotion overcame her so quickly that she thought for a moment she might faint. Although Kathleen never swore in front of her parents, she hadn't even noticed that she had. She just stared at her father, waiting for him to tell her she was wrong, that the list was not what she had imagined. Those words never came. The silence was remarkably uncomfortable for both of them, but finally Mr. DelGiorno spoke.

"Kathleen, you have to understand it is not like it looks. These people came to me. It was their choice for themselves."

He went on to explain how he had accomplished it, hoping that by her understanding it was done humanely, perhaps she would forgive him or at least be more sympathetic about why he was involved. Once a person had made the arrangements with him and given him a deposit of half the money, he would give them three to four Vicodin pills to save until the day they were ready. They would call and set a time with Mr. DelGiorno. Once they had taken the pills and been rendered unconscious, only then would he inject the two ounces of Cav-all into their veins that would kill them, usually rather quickly, with no terrible side effects.

So many thoughts and questions raced through her mind she didn't even know where to start, or worse, if she wanted to know more. "What does it have to do with me? Why did they each come to me too? Did I somehow incite their death?"

"Kathleen, that is not possible. Other than Mrs. Delabarto, every one of them had made the call to me themselves when they were ready. It was their choice. It was just an assisted suicide, not a cold-blooded murder," he explained, then hesitated briefly before continuing.

"The only reason that Mrs. Delabarto had not called herself was she became incapacitated very quickly, but she had left word with her eldest son to contact me if something happened to her."

He went on to explain how he had thought of the idea after Jack Kevorkian's operations had been shut down and then reading up on Death with Dignity laws that had been passed in other states, but it was a couple of years later before he actually acted on it. He had been dealing with sick people and death nearly all his life and agreed with Mr. Kevorkian's willingness to help with euthanasia. Providing a dignified death was what he considered his work to be.

He studied humane ways to carry out his plan then with the help of a close hospice staff member was given referrals that consisted of the names Kathleen had discovered on the list. It worked out well because they usually would also make a prearrangement right along with their death arrangements. He could count only a few who had not used the firm at the time of their deaths.

"Well, what about Mr. O'Brien? If it was so humane, why the hell did he get out of bed and die in the kitchen? Dad, do you realize what you are telling me?"

It dawned on her that this was why his wife was so calm, and it explained also why she had thanked them on their way out of the house. She was expecting his death. Knowing this totally crept Kathleen out.

Mr. DelGiorno explained that perhaps he had misjudged the amount of Vicodin needed to put him out, or maybe Mr. O'Brien had not taken the right amount of sedative himself. "Mrs. Updike, she wasn't even sick, Dad. I could better understand a terminal patient, but why someone who was not even sick?"

"Marion was getting old, and she had no children to take care of her. She was going to be forced to go to a nursing home, and she did not want to live like that. She had eighty great years, and she was ready to go with her pride still intact."

Over the years, just a few who were not terminally ill had contacted him. He avoided them in most cases but recently had also assisted Mr. Carter because he had been so lost since his wife had died. Although not physically terminal, mentally he was.

Kathleen could feel her face burning, and although she was hot, chills kept running through her body. She did not know whether to feel sorry for him or to hate him at this moment. What he was saying was logical, but it all was against everything she had ever been taught by him. She had never been faced with such a rational set of absurd explanations. The list of what she considered participating victims kept rolling through her mind.

"What about Mr. Thomas? He was your friend, Dad. He was a friend to all of us. You acted so devastated at the funeral—that is just wrong."

"Kathleen, you know that I loved Mr. Thomas dearly, which is exactly why I helped him when he needed me most."

Based on what he was saying and how he was justifying his actions, he clearly believed it to be right. This was what his people wanted, and he explained most had arranged it for themselves with the exception of a few families who knew their loved one would not want to live in the misery of sickness. He felt that it was his duty. That it was just another service he could provide to his families to help them ease their suffering. Torn between the moralities of doing the right thing and ensuring his families needs were met at all costs.

Kathleen began to rationalize his words to herself. Assisting another in a death that they chose, was that really so bad? It was not like he was a cold-blooded murderer, someone who took innocent lives with no warning. He and his clients—if that was what you would call them—simply wanted a dignified way to die. Wasn't that their choice? Kathleen's crazy thoughts of justification continued for minutes and then rolled back to the finality that it still wasn't right, and she could not condone what he had done. Not to mention it was illegal, so no matter what people thought, he would still need to be held accountable. Her dad could tell by the look on her face that the conversation would be ending. His eyes showed his sheer regret for disappointing his family. "Have you told anyone?" he asked, still composed like the rock he always was.

"Johnny and I have discussed it, but he is the only one so far. Dad, I am going to have to tell. I can't stand by and support this."

"I would never expect you to. It is something that I still believe is right but always knew that others may not feel the same. I have made my choices for my reasons, and you have to make yours for your own reasons. You know that is what I have always supported, your right to make your own mind up. Your strong will is one of your best traits. Please though, give me a couple of days to get some things in order for you and your mother, and then you can do what you feel is right."

"I can do that. I love you, Daddy!"

She walked over and embraced her father, and they both began to cry. They held on to each other for a long while, and Kathleen felt protected by him. He was a noble man and was true to everyone he came in contact with. She admired that and hoped that his reputation would be what got her family through this. She needed some time to think and decided that she could not do that with her mom or dad nearby.

She passed through the funeral home to grab the extra keys to the Cadillac, and as she headed toward the garage, her eyes met the neatly framed copy of the Funeral Director's Oath. She knew that same strong commitment that forced her father to so often turn his back on his own family out of necessity to meet the needs of others was what had been so long engrained in her. This time, she must turn her back on him to ensure she upheld the nobility and laws of the profession. After all, it was the oath she had taken just about year ago. Ultimately she was going to have to tell in order to protect the families of those she vowed to serve. She left the house not knowing at all where she would go but just knowing that she needed time to think. Time to get away from making this choice.

As she drove aimlessly, she thought about calling Mimi. It had been a couple of days, and she hadn't yet returned her call, but she really didn't want to talk to her. It would force her to talk about the wedding. A topic she'd rather avoid because right now, she didn't even know if her own father would be at the wedding once this story broke.

Kath never really went anywhere; she just drove without direction, through street after street, searching for something she would never find. Perhaps, something to provide peace of mind. A sign to indicate what she should do. A premonition that all would be just fine. If she was going to be a clairvoyant, she would much rather be seeing good endings. But the real answer was always there. She just hoped in vain something would change her mind.

As Kathleen finally rolled into the driveway, she was relieved that every light in the house was off. She wouldn't have to face anyone. Too much guilt to face her mother, too much disappointment to face her dad. She wanted nothing more than to crawl into bed and sleep for days. If only she could figure out how to get away with it.

She undressed and pulled on her most comfortable pj's. These were the ones she always chose when she had a bad day. The fluffy pink material seemed to wrap around her almost like a hug, and she desperately needed that right now. She quietly wandered to the bathroom to brush her teeth, dreading the possibility that someone might awaken and want to talk. She was in no condition to see either of her parents. She knew that eye contact with either one would mean an instant breakdown.

She flicked on the bathroom light and closed the door just halfway. Grabbed what she needed from the drawer and glanced into the mirror. Her eyes looked like giant red superballs, puffed nearly double in side. She was glad she had decided not to go see Johnny. He certainly wouldn't have wanted to hold her close tonight, not with her looking like a bad mix between a vampire from *Twilight* and Ozzy Osbourne. She laughed to herself then let out a grateful sigh that she had been lucky enough to land him.

She brushed well, top first, then bottom, then a swish of mouthwash. At least her breath felt fresh even though no other part of her did. She let the water run to very cold and splashed it over her face in hopes of taking down some of the swelling. She reached around blindly for the towel and ever so gently raised her head to take one last look. As she made contact with her face in the mirror, there was another face.

There behind her at the door was her dad. *Shit! He caught me awake, now what will I say?* She turned to speak, but there was no one. *Go to bed,* she ordered. *You are damn tired, and you are playing mind games with yourself. He probably doesn't want to see me either.* She laughed at herself for being so paranoid in her own home and moved swiftly to her room while avoiding any more contact with mirrors.

She found her phone and set it on a low ringtone near her nightstand, next to the funeral home landline. Enough to wake her but not enough to completely startle her in the event a call came in overnight. She texted Johnny good night and was out before her head hit the pillow.

FINAL CHAPTER

Even after turning her phone down, Kathleen still awoke startled by the noise of the phone ringing so early in the morning. At least it was probably not a death call, because it was coming in on her cell. Death calls usually went to the funeral home phone or her dad's cell first.

She noticed Johnny's number right away and was a little miffed he'd be calling so damn early, knowing how she was feeling and what time she had finally gotten to bed last night. Even though it was just Johnny, she still tried to sound wide awake, something she learned about answering phones from her dad. "Hey, what's up?" she questioned, trying to act as if she wasn't put out by his early phone call.

"Kathleen, I need you to bring the hearse to Dead Man's Curve right away."

"Do we have a call? Do I need my dad?"

"Yes and no," he instructed rather insistently. She wondered why but continued to listen since there was such urgency in his voice.

"You don't need your dad. Just you, bring a cot and come right away. I will give you the details when you get here."

"Okay, I need a few minutes to dress and compose myself, but I'll hurry."

Johnny better be in the mood to help with a removal if she wasn't bringing her dad. No one at Dead Man's Curve was ever in very good shape. Why such urgency? She figured maybe it was someone that lived on that road, and they wanted to clear the scene before a family member drove by on the way to work or school. Either way, she hurried along as she had been instructed, trying very hard not to wake her parents. She still didn't want to see them and figured this little escape would help put off the inevitable at least for a little longer.

As she drove toward Huckabee Road, she continued to contemplate what to do next about her dad. It really was wrong no matter how he justified it, and she couldn't comfortably work and live at that funeral home, knowing about her dad's little side business. Yet she felt a commitment to him and her mother who had taken such good care of her all her life. She pressed the gas a little harder just get to the scene, where she could focus on someone else's misfortune for a while.

The sun was just peeking above the horizon, a new day for many but not for this person. She said a little prayer for the family as she came closer to the scene.

As she rounded the corner, there were many emergency vehicles on site. She could see Johnny moving swiftly toward the hearse. Just as she brought the hearse to a slow halt, her eyes finally had a panoramic view of the wreck at the big oak. The mangled mess was almost unrecognizable but she clearly could make out the license plate *9 3 5 S L H* on the black Cadillac smashed headfirst into the tree. She knew then it was the family car from the funeral home.

Tears welled in her eyes. She knew now why Johnny did not want her to wake her dad. She couldn't—he was gone. She couldn't even open the door because that would mean she must face what was out there. She tried to snap out of it, wake herself from this ridiculous dream, but Johnny's obnoxious pounding on the window was all too real. This was not a dream, this was death in the raw, and it was her dad.

She finally managed to put the car in park, which in turn released the locks, and then Johnny quickly opened the door and grabbed her. So many thoughts ran through her mind. What was disappointment yesterday kept moving back and forth to guilt, then misery, then on to anger. It seemed she was experiencing the five stages of grief in an instant.

Was this really an accident, was he so ashamed of his actions that he took his own life, or was he protecting her and her mother from the despair of a trial and conviction? She guessed the latter. How could she be mad at that? The business could go on without having marred the name and ruining any chance of success for Kathleen. That was how noble he was. He knew that it was his responsibility to help her make up her mind. He would relieve her and her mother of the pain and remove the disgrace it would cause the funeral home.

Now she did not have to tell anyone. The investigation would stall because there would be no more deaths. She knew that she could trust Johnny not to tell now, not when Kath and her mother would have this great burden to bear. Kathleen was sure that her dad had counted on the fact that she would protect her mother from knowing all the details. That she would pretend that this was really a freak accident, just like everyone else at the scene thought—except, of course, her and Johnny.

This reassurance gave her enough strength to begin to shift from family member to funeral director, although she left the removal to the coroners on scene. Joe and Johnny were more than willing to help in this case. She even let them load the cot but insisted on closing the door herself.

The door of the hearse closed loudly, the finality of it announcing the last ride for Mr. DelGiorno.

She would contact Roger once she got back to the funeral home in hopes that if he wouldn't do the embalming, he would be able to recommend someone else. She knew that she would not be able to do it herself.

"Joe, I am going to ride back with Kathleen. I will be back to the office soon."

He knew that he would have to help Kathleen tell her mother. He wouldn't want them to be alone. He now was going to be the man of the house, and he wondered if Mr. DelGiorno felt more comfortable with his decision to bury this secret knowing his family would be taken care of. He would never know for sure.

Joe responded with a kindness always present in his actions. "If you hadn't suggested it, I would have, son. Go on ahead, and if you need more time, just call the office. I will take care of it."

Kathleen slowly began to drive away from the scene using her side mirrors to guide her moves. Then she looked straight into the rearview mirror to check her status. She still hoped it was all a mistake, a nightmare. She hoped maybe her dad would be sitting up, smiling at her in the back, giving her some reassurance that he was okay. No such luck. All she could see was the bulked-up cot and country road behind her, beaming with the springtime sun and bright-green buds that had just recently began to bloom upon the trees. The dust from the road swirled as if it were dancing. The tune "I can see clearly now the rain has gone" echoed ever so softly through her head. As she continued looking back, she was certain that the rearview mirror would give her no more troubles. Those secrets were going to the grave.

Jules Chicken Divine

    2 boneless skinless chicken breasts cooked and diced in to
    bite size pieces
    1 can cream of mushroom soup
    1 cup mayonnaise
    1 egg
    1 box frozen chopped broccoli (thawed and drained)
    12 oz. of shredded sharp white cheddar cheese

Mix all ingredients in large oven safe bowl. Bake at 350 degrees for
45 minutes. Serve over rice. Makes 4 servings.

ABOUT THE AUTHOR

A lifelong resident of Upstate New York, K.C. Long wrote her debut novel, *Looking Back,* after changing careers. A former funeral director, she was eager to preserve some of the most interesting, touching, and sometimes crazy stories from her work in the field. Now a primary school teacher, after teaching a writing lesson one day, her students were the just inspiration she needed to begin work on her novel and create a fascinating story for others to enjoy.

CPSIA information can be obtained
at www.ICGtesting.com
Printed in the USA
FFOW03n0303101017
40913FF

9 781640 276406